TAKING STEPS

Towhay is an old manor house on the edge of a small English village. Ross is a hard-headed executive whose only aim in life, it seems, is to make money. When he buys Towhay from Elizabeth, who's in financial difficulties, he plans to turn it into an exclusive hotel. Elizabeth's friend, Gillian, owns the village tea shop. She firmly believes that other things are more important than making money. So, will Ross and Gillian resolve their differences and perhaps find love and commitment?

WENDY KREMER

TAKING STEPS

Complete and Unabridged

LINFORD
Leicester

First published in Great Britain in 2010

First Linford Edition
published 2011

British Library CIP Data

Kremer, Wendy.
    Taking steps. - -
    (Linford romance library)
    1. Real estate developers- -Fiction.
    2. Villages- -England- -Fiction.
    3. Love stories. 4. Large type books.
    I. Title II. Series
    823.9'2–dc22

    ISBN 978–1–4448–0921–3

Published by

1

Ross Harley was sitting at one of the window tables, deeply engrossed in some papers. Busy making coffee and arranging the scones, cream and jam on delicate white china, Gillian Churchill glanced at him out of the corner of her eye.

Her tea shop called Something's Brewing was well-known locally, but the village was not on a main highway and it seldom attracted strangers.

Gillian brought him his order. Handsome with a beautifully proportioned body, his profile was strong and rigid. He looked up briefly and, with a reserved expression, nodded his thanks. His features were symmetrical; the inherent strength and sharpness of his face was softened by doggy-brown eyes and sandy-coloured hair that just brushed the collar of his business suit.

Gillian decided he was someone who knew just how to get what he wanted from life.

Moving back behind the old-fashioned wooden counter, she began to empty the dishwasher and then stack freshly ironed tablecloths in the old cupboard in the corner. The only other customers were the vicar's wife, and Ellie Thomson; they were tucked away in one of the shadowy corners. A grandfather clock marked the passing minutes with a loud ticking sound. She couldn't help looking at the stranger from time to time. He was munching one of her scones and, apart from occasionally looking at his watch and glancing at the village green, his whole attention was focussed on the papers in front of him. He had large hands, long fingers and neat nails. Gillian looked at the clock uneasily and was relieved when the tinkle of the bell announced Jean's arrival.

Slightly breathless, Jean rushed over. 'Sorry, love! I planned to be here sooner, but Mum called at the last minute and you know how difficult it is to get rid of her when she gets on her hobby-horse about the church flowers!'

Gillian lifted a warning finger, nodding in the direction of the customers in the corner. 'No problem! I'll go by Wilmot's field, be there in plenty of time.'

Jean trailed after her, into the tiny hallway that led from the café into the small kitchen, and also to the narrow stairs to Gillian's small flat. Over her shoulder, as she took the steps at a run, Gillian said. 'There's a batch of scone mixture ready, if you need it. Oh! — the man at the window table hasn't paid yet. Coffee and scones!'

Ten minutes later, with her make-up renewed and wearing a straight skirt instead of trousers, she waved to Jean who was serving a newly arrived customer and hurried out. The stranger had already left, too. It was a bright September day, full of sunlight. Apart from the twittering of the birds in the bordering hedges, it was blissfully quiet. According to her watch, she still had plenty of time, but she increased her pace, not wishing to be late. The fields climbed gradually and the dying stubble from the summer harvest was still evident. The air was cool with the scent of the earth and the countryside. Gillian loved it here; she couldn't imagine living anywhere else.

The breeze played with her ash-blonde hair. It was straight and short, and cut closely to the shape of her head. Her eyes were greenish-blue and seemed to change colour according to her surroundings and her mood. As she approached the crest of the field, she paused and looked downhill to Towhay. What a magnificent Elizabethan manor house it was. She hadn't got used to the idea that it might soon belong to someone else. She'd been visiting Towhay, and its owner Elizabeth Taunton, ever since she could remember. Despite the difference in age, they

4

were firm friends.

She began to walk down quickly and ended up running helter-skelter until she reached the gardens. She went in through the back door, passed through the panelled grand entrance hall with its fine open fireplace, and went towards the drawing room overlooking the gardens. Gillian guessed Elizabeth would take her visitor there, and she was right. She heard voices before she knocked.

Elizabeth smiled warmly. 'Ah, Gillian! There you are! Come in! This is Mr Ross Harley. He owns Dreamhotels — the company that's interested in buying Towhay.'

Gillian returned Elizabeth's smile and held out her hand to Mr Harley, the man who'd been devouring her scones a short time ago. 'Good morning! I'm Elizabeth's friend.' Confidently she continued. 'She asked me to be present, I hope you don't mind?'

He took her hand; his handshake was warm and firm. 'No, of course not! We met just now — in the village — didn't we?'

'Yes, in my teashop. I'm Gillian Churchill. Please don't let me interrupt.' Gillian moved to the window seat and sat out of the way, with her ankles neatly crossed. She paid attention to the conversation but didn't comment. She was an alert and interested listener because she wanted to support Elizabeth and ensure that, even if Elizabeth was forced by circumstances to make one of the most important decisions of her life, she'd be happy with the outcome of Ross Harley's proposals and information.

It gave her time to study Ross Harley again. Apart from his polite greeting when she arrived, he disregarded her. He gave Elizabeth his whole attention. Gillian realised that he knew she had no say in the final decision, so he could afford to ignore her, and he did. He painstakingly explained his plans for Towhay to Elizabeth.

Gillian had always loved Elizabeth's

house; it was a romantic place, a source of constant peace and contentment — or it had been until this man arrived. His scheme would change everything; not just for the house, things would change locally too. She opposed the idea of him turning Towhay into a luxury hotel, but she also knew that Elizabeth was finding it impossible to cope with the repairs and the cost of its upkeep. It would in fact be a godsend in the long run if Towhay was rescued from degenerating into a neglected and derelict state. Elizabeth had one great nephew, but he had absolutely no interest in Towhay. When the time came, he'd put it up for sale before Elizabeth was cold in her grave.

Gillian could tell that Elizabeth was warming to Ross Harley, and Ross Harley was using all his charm to convince Elizabeth that selling the house would be the right decision. His voice broke into Gillian's meanderings. He was handing Elizabeth some glossy brochures.

'I thought you might like to see some of our other hotels. We try to retain the original appearances and atmosphere of the various buildings as far as it is possible. Any necessary changes and modifications are done by a team of experts. We aim to make the buildings luxurious residences, perfect places to stay for anyone who can afford the price.' He fanned the brochures out on the table. 'Here you can see some other conversions. A Georgian manor house, a medieval century castle in Tuscany, a seventeenth century inn in Provence, a former private home on the island of Jersey, a small city hotel in Paris and an ex-working farmhouse in north Wales. They all have top-class restaurant facilities, spa and treatment suites and are either four or five star hotels.'

'Spa? That probably means a swimming pool, doesn't it? Where would you put a swimming pool in Towhay?' Elizabeth's dainty features were animated. She smiled at him and waited.

His smile matched Elizabeth's in its

8

liveliness, and Gillian reminded herself that she didn't like the reason this man was here.

'You have several large unused outhouses. I'm sure a clever designer could make a fantastic spa area in one of those. I thought we could also use the stables again, install someone local, and simply let them run their business from here. They could hire their horses out to hotel visitors on request — a kind of symbiosis!'

Gillian immediately thought of her friend Caroline. At the moment, Caroline had her stables in a rundown building and her lease was running out next year. She didn't say anything, but she was sure Caroline would jump at the chance of moving from her present shabby surroundings into the stables at Towhay.

Elizabeth's blue eyes twinkled and she sounded almost cheerful. 'I like that idea very much. I don't think the stables have been used as such since the beginning of the Second World War!'

She picked up the brochures, glanced at them and handed them to Gillian.

Gillian flipped through the glossy leaflets and had to admit the hotels looked good. If alterations had taken place, they'd been done with maximum attention to authenticity.

Ross Harley was folded into one of Elizabeth's soft chintz-covered sofas. Even though his long frame was probably used to firmer support, he still managed to look at ease in his made-to-measure business suit. Despite her resolve to remain neutral, Gillian admitted that his self-confidence and clean looks impressed her, and they seemed to impress Elizabeth too.

Elizabeth was in her seventies, but she knew exactly which questions to put. 'Who exactly is Dreamhotels, Mr Harley? I like to know who my negotiating partners are. I don't like anonymity!'

Tongue in cheek, his dark eyes twinkled. 'I'm Dreamhotels. I'm your negotiating partner; there is no one else. I've one managing director, but I'm sole owner of the company.'

Elizabeth looked at him with respect. 'Then you must be a very wealthy young man.'

A grin overtook his features. 'It seems that way, doesn't it — but wealth is relative when most of it is tied up in contracts and words. I started out with the farmhouse in north Wales, and when it paid its way, I used the profit to finance the second scheme, and so on.'

Elizabeth nodded and asked shrewdly, 'If you use the success of one to finance your next step, there is a danger it might all topple like a pack of cards — and then Towhay might end up back on the market again. I wouldn't like that to happen.'

He laughed softly. 'I can't give you a 100% guarantee Miss Taunton, who can? But I do own a couple of these hotels outright now, and I promise that the likelihood of me losing some, or all of them, is not very likely — we do too much market research for that and don't take risks. As you can imagine, exclusive hotels are expensive to run, but they make a profit if they are run properly and on a long-term basis. When the asking price of one is paid off, I either lean back and live from the income, or search for a new project and expand. I was tempted again when I found Towhay was up for sale. It's a beautiful house, and it would suit our purposes exactly. It's a gem of an Elizabethan manor house!'

★　★　★

A few weeks later, on market day, Gillian was serving some customers when the bell over the door announced a new arrival. She looked up and her normally pale face coloured. Ross Harley ducked his head under the lintel, looked around and covered the intervening distance quickly. His hands were thrust into the pockets of his soft camel-hair overcoat. His deep voice was loud enough for her to hear above the hum of the room. 'I know that you're busy, but if you have a minute, I'd like a word with you.'

Gillian looked up at him; the surprise of seeing him again was beginning to fade. She glanced around quickly. 'I'm about to serve that table in the corner, then I can spare you a few moments, but not very long. Today is market day, and we're always very busy!'

Ross leaned on the counter and watched her, a gleam of interest in his eyes. On her return, he followed her into the small hallway. He was so big that he filled the space, and her nerves tensed. She straightened her shoulders and waited. He didn't keep her in doubt for long.

'I know your word carries a lot of weight with Miss Taunton. I was wondering if you'd put in a good word for me, about selling?'

His cheek nearly took her breath away. She threw him a cold stare. 'Why should I? Elizabeth is perfectly capable

13

of deciding for herself. I've no intention of trying to influence her.'

His dark eyebrow lifted. 'You must admit that under the circumstances, and considering her age, it'd be a very wise move — in my opinion the only sensible move.'

He acted as if there was no alternative, and Gillian felt annoyed. 'Even if I do agree wholeheartedly with what you say, I won't pressure her, one way or the other. She's my friend; an old lady who has a medieval house that's the centre of her whole life. It's only thanks to her exertions that the house is still in a half-way acceptable state. She has no close family and a rapidly dwindling income, otherwise I'm sure she would have preferred to stay there until she died.'

With the sense of conviction that was part of his character, he answered casually. 'Then it would be a shrewd move for you to encourage her to sell now. I promise that Towhay will get the care and attention it needs.'

She met his eyes boldly and tried hard to retain her affability. 'Sorry, but no! I won't interfere! Elizabeth must decide for herself without any recommendation from me.'

He studied her and then nodded. If he was annoyed, it didn't show, apart from a brief glint in those dark brown eyes. He looked around the tiny kitchen and remarked, 'You've a nice little business here. Lots of customers and a going concern.'

She was still irked by his attempt to get her to influence Elizabeth and had to clench her mouth in an attempt to stay cool; but she matched his light tone. 'Yes. We're off the main highway, but once the word got around, it worked. We now have lots of loyal customers.'

'I was just thinking — if you extended the space, put in some more tables, you'd increase your turnover. You make your own cakes and so on, don't you? Perhaps it'd pay to contract that sort of thing out?'

She glared at him and her cheeks reddened. Bristling, she kept her voice casual, but cool. 'If I ever want your expert opinion about my teashop, Mr Harley, I'll ask for it. If I tried to upgrade Something's Brewing, I'm sure it would be half-empty most days. People like the tearoom because of its little nooks and crannies; they don't mind if it's a bit cramped. Our cakes and scones go down well just because they're home-made. If I don't have time to make everything myself, I have some people who make me cakes on demand.' She threw back her head in a gesture of defiance. 'If you'll excuse me now, I have customers to serve!'

There was a glint of amusement in his eyes when he answered, tongue in cheek, 'I like the name of the place — although I suppose it might be associated with witches and the like! I must confess I understand why you're so busy — your scones are first-class.' He made a sweeping gesture with his hand. 'Don't let me keep you any longer!'

She didn't comment and he followed her back into the bustle of the small room. Grabbing her pad and pencil, she hurried to serve some new arrivals.

Some of the customers paused in their gossiping to give the tall, good-looking stranger a second glance. Gillian would have been surprised to see him exit with the expression of someone who was satisfied.

Ross's visit had merely been to discover if she planned to sway Elizabeth Taunton's decision against him. Clearly she didn't. Towhay's owner and this girl were close, and if Gillian Churchill did express disapproval, it would make things infinitely more difficult for him. He looked at his watch. He'd visit Elizabeth Taunton again and see if he could clear any remaining doubts. He got into his silver BMW, looked through the windscreen at the old-fashioned teashop and grudgingly admired the girl's attitude. She was clearly sceptical about him. She barely reached his shoulder, but she knew how to express herself and was in all probability a temperamental adversary!

2

Elizabeth had accepted Ross' bid for
Towhay, and she and Gillian were
wandering. They went from the living
room, into the dining room with its
Elizabethan and Jacobean panelling and
impressive chimney piece, then through
some other reception rooms and the
well stocked library with its mass of
leather backed books before they
climbed the carved staircase. Gillian
thought about the games of hide-and-
seek she'd played here with other village
children, the carol singers in the main
entrance hall at Christmas time, the
sunbeams drifting through the diamond
windowpanes to make patterns on the
flagged floor in high summer. She loved
it almost as much as Elizabeth did.

'You'll feel wretched about leaving,'
she told Elizabeth. 'I would!' She
wondered what it would all look like

when Ross Harley had finished his modifications. Most of the rooms were unused these days, but Elizabeth and Jenny, her help from the village, had striven to keep things in a habitable state. Money invested by Elizabeth's father in better times had sufficed to keep things running until the combination of storm damage, and declining interest rates, had forced Elizabeth into her present position.

Upstairs there was another large reception room and an array of bedrooms, each with a connected dressing room. Gillian mused that these would be perfect for en-suite bathrooms. The rooms in the extensive attics had been populated by servants in earlier times; and perhaps some of them might end up as employees' rooms again. As long as Gillian could remember, they'd only been gathering dust. Most of the bedrooms had wonderful views over the remains of the gardens and the surrounding countryside beyond.

Gazing out of a window, Gillian

looked down on the old dairy, a detached stone and brick building, the former stables, the long-unused Victorian glasshouse and various other outhouses. The gardens had been very extensive long ago, but were now limited to what Elizabeth and the two part-time gardeners could manage. They'd succeeded in maintaining the Knot Garden with an apple tree at its centre, and a large rose garden with beautiful scented roses chosen entirely for their perfume.

Gillian was aware that a whole era was coming to an end and she felt a great sadness. Elizabeth must be feeling utterly miserable. Gillian turned, and their eyes met.

Elizabeth moved to stand next to her, patting Gillian's arm. 'Don't worry; I'll manage. In some ways, it will be a relief. I have the feeling that Ross Harley will maintain the best of the place. I've studied the brochures about his places and read all about them — he has never radically changed anything he owns. He even deliberately kept period features like wonky floors in some places. I have to be sensible — I can't take care of Towhay properly, you know that. If the house is an exclusive, well-cared for hotel in the future, then I'll be half-way happy to know that it'll survive, even though it won't be a home any more. Randall doesn't give a jot about the place; never has. He wouldn't try to rescue it even if I gave it to him, so it's my duty to put it into good hands now.'

She sighed. 'If I'd married and had children, the story might have been different, but the war put an end to all that.' She shrugged and continued. 'I think Ross is a level-headed business-man, and he wouldn't take on a house like Towhay unless he is fairly sure he can make a success of it.'

'And you're sure you want to stay locally? You're not afraid of knowing that Towhay is just down the road but that it belongs to someone else?'

Elizabeth smiled. 'No, I don't think

I'll mind once I've adjusted to the idea. I can keep an eye on it from afar. Ross says I can even look around whenever I want to. I don't intend to do so very often, but it will be nice to wander through Towhay now and then.'

'He's a businessman to the core isn't he?'

Elizabeth looked thoughtful: 'Yes, I agree — but everything has its price. In the course of the conversation the other day, Fiona told me he was in love with someone years ago, but kept putting off making a serious commitment. When he considered he was successful enough to think of other things, it was too late. She'd already married someone else, and on top of that, she was killed in a car accident a short time later. Fiona says it softened his attitude to work, but he's still driven by ambition and big business.'

Gillian, startled by this, changed the subject. 'And what happens now?'

'The lawyers take over and I have to find somewhere else to live. The agreement allows me to take what furniture I want with me, and they keep the rest. I do hope most of it will stay in Towhay. In a strange way, I find the whole business quite exciting. I also think I'll be glad to lay down the burden of looking after it, once I've settled somewhere else. I love Towhay deeply, I always will, you know that — but it needs more than I can give it any more. Someone else, with money, has to take over.'

'You'll have no say in what's altered, or how it's done?'

She shook her head. 'From what Ross told me, the exterior remains more or less untouched, and the knot garden and rose garden will stay put too. Lots of things connected with the house are probably under conservation rules, so no one can go completely haywire. This isn't the first time he's done a conversion. The main changes will be in making bathrooms, installing an efficient kitchen, creating the swimming pool and spa, that sort of thing.'

Gillian wavered, but decided now was as good a time as ever. 'Danny Warden's cottage is up for sale; I wondered if it might suit you? It's not very big, but it has two bedrooms, two fair-sized down-stairs rooms and a small kitchen. As you know, he was a keen gardener, so it already has a decent garden. It's also in a good state of repair.'

Elizabeth's eyes lit up hopefully. 'Is it? I didn't know that. It's a sweet little cottage, all those paned windows and overhanging roof. I'd love to live in the village. Do you think I can look around? I presumed that one of Danny's relatives would want it.'

'No, they just want money! If you like, I'll phone the estate agent, ask when you can view. If you don't like it, we'll be sure to find something else nearby that you do. How much time do you have to find a new home?'

'Ross said I could take as long as I need. Planning permission has to be sorted out, and that takes time. Appar-ently, there's a great deal of organisation to sort out before they can actually start working. I want to be out before they start altering things, though.'

★   ★   ★

Once Elizabeth had looked around the vacant cottage she was eager to buy it — and she had to find the money to buy it as fast as she could, because several other people were interested.

Gillian rang Ross' office number; Elizabeth had given her his business card. Gillian didn't like phoning him, but Elizabeth's worries had priority over what she felt about the man.

'Fiona Burroughs — Dreamhotels. Can I help you?' The voice was efficient but not unfriendly.

Gillian hadn't reckoned with talking to an assistant; she adjusted her approach. 'Good morning! My name is Gillian Churchill; I'd like to speak to Mr Harley, please.' There was a silent pause; the name clearly meant nothing to her; Gillian hastened to add. 'I want to talk to him about Towhay. I'm speaking on behalf of Miss Elizabeth Taunton.

There was a definite softening of her manner. 'Oh, I see! Mr Harley's not here at the moment. He's away on business, in Tuscany. Can I help?'

Gillian bit her lip. Illogically, she was irritated because he was out of reach when he was needed. 'No, it's personal. Perhaps you'll tell him I phoned?'

'Yes, of course. Does he have your number?'

'No.' She gave it and Fiona repeated it.

'I'll tell him you called next time he contacts me, Miss Churchill.'

Gillian wondered when that would be, but didn't ask. 'Thank you.' She put down the phone and admitted that her negative view of Ross Harley was illogical. She ran her hand over her ash-blonde hair and looked at her pale pink-tipped fingers. She wasn't being reasonable — even Ross Harley deserved a chance.

Later that evening, she was enjoying some peace and quiet. The café had been closed for several hours. She'd made two cakes for tomorrow's display stand, and phoned Jean's mother to also supply them with a carrot cake, and a chocolate gateau tomorrow to round off the choice. She made her own fresh scones every day according to needs, and only increased her cake selection from outside sources on special days, or holiday times — as circumstances demanded.

Soft yellow light bathed the small sitting room and its comfortable furniture. Soft swing music bounced through the air and there was an open book on her lap. Her legs were tucked up on the sofa under a lightweight rug and she was thoroughly enjoying a well-earned cup of tea. The sound of the phone startled her.

'Gillian? — I may call you Gillian, I hope? Fiona gave me your message and said you wanted to talk to me?'

The sound of his deep voice on her

telephone made something inside her flutter. How silly! 'Oh, hello Mr Harley — or, rather, Ross! I didn't expect to hear from you at this time of night.'

With a note of amusement in his voice, he replied. 'Am I disturbing you?'

'No, no — of course not! I didn't mean that.' She pulled herself together and started to explain. A minute or so later, she recapped, 'So you see if the bank doesn't get some kind of assurance that money is on the horizon, they won't cover for financing Elizabeth's cottage.'

'Hmm! As far as I know, the lawyers are still working on the small print. Until that's completed, and Elizabeth's lawyers have given it the go ahead, I don't officially need to push any money over the counter.' He was silent for a second. 'But I understand why she needs some fluid cash now.' There was another short pause. 'I'll give the bank my personal guarantee that the money is forthcoming, and if they don't accept that, I'll make her a personal loan. She can pay it back when the deal goes through.'

Gillian hesitated, then said. 'The cottage isn't cheap.'

He gave a soft laugh. 'I can imagine! What's cheap these days? Do you have the bank details — the address, the account number, or such?'

Gillian fumbled with one hand in her handbag, lying next to the sofa. 'I know the address and the sorting number, because I bank with them too. I didn't think to ask Elizabeth for her account number, but her family has banked there from time immemorial, they're sure to know who you're talking about if you mention her name.' Gillian spun out the address and the other details of the bank. 'It would be a great help. Elizabeth is so worried in case someone else snaps up the cottage from under her nose. She was too embarrassed to ask you, so I took it out of her hands. Thank — thank you for being so considerate.'

'Tell her not to worry. I'll sort the bank manager out tomorrow and he'll be in touch with Elizabeth.'

Gillian felt certain he'd soon have the bank manager turning somersaults. She decided she ought to be polite and affable, he was about to do Elizabeth a big favour. 'Your assistant said you are in Tuscany?'

'Yes. At this moment, I'm sitting in the inner courtyard of our castello and I have a very good Barolo wine in front of me. The temperatures are mild and the sunset is amazing!'

Gillian had an impulse to tell him how the other half lived. 'Lucky you! I'm lounging on a saggy sofa in my living room, the sun hasn't shown itself all day, and I'm drinking a cup of lukewarm PG!'

There was a couple of seconds of silence and then a soft laugh on the other end of the line. 'You may be surprised, but that sounds pretty good too! Night, Gillian.'

'Goodnight! And thank you again

— I'm sure Elizabeth will be extremely grateful.'

There was a click and the connection was broken.

★   ★   ★

Elizabeth glanced around the small cottage with a pleased expression on her face. 'It looks lovely! I nearly had a heart attack when your Dad started to pull everything about. The new bathroom is beautiful. The one I had in Towhay was big enough for a horse to bath in, but it was always cold, and especially in winter.'

Gillian's father owned a small building firm. He'd persuaded Elizabeth to renew the drainage, the electric wiring and to revamp the bathroom completely before she moved in. When Elizabeth saw the initial chaos she was very uneasy, but now she was excited because the cottage looked impressive. Gillian, Elizabeth and Gillian's mum were currently decorating the rooms whenever they had time to spare.

Everything was now almost finished and Elizabeth was clearing up, and preparing to go home. 'Did I mention Ross came down a couple of days ago? He wanted to see the cottage, and we came here together. He said he understood why I'd chosen it.'

Gillian's mind was suddenly working overtime with images of Ross Harley. 'Did he? When do you expect to exchange contracts?'

'Soon.' Elizabeth stroked the smooth white surface of one of the shallow window sills. 'I've started to think about which furniture I'd like to take with me. I'm restricted because of the size, and I need to choose some nice smaller pieces that fit in here. But it's hard for me to imagine what does and what doesn't fit.'

'Why don't we draw a sketch of the rooms, measure the furniture you like, and see if it all fits in as you expect on paper first? I expect my dad has some millimetre paper. We could do it one day next week, if you like. We've finished the painting work apart from this hall — and I'll be finished with that too before I go.'

Elizabeth clapped her hands like a child. 'Oh, yes! That's a good idea. I'm not good at judging sizes!' She took hold of Gillian's shoulders and kissed her gently on her cheek. 'Oh Gillian, you have been so good to me; I would have been lost without your help. Thank you.'

Gillian had a lump in her throat. 'I'm happy to help, you know that. You're my third granny!'

Elizabeth left her to go home and Gillian stayed to finish off painting the hall. A small portable radio was a pleasant companion. An hour or so later, she stood back with her hands on her hips to view the results of her effort. The walls were now a pale eggshell blue. Gillian could imagine the little hallway with some of Elizabeth's paintings, and some pieces of small-sized furniture. She didn't hear him enter, so when she turned and came face to face with Ross, she jumped. She opened her mouth and shut it; frowning, she snapped, 'Good heavens! You gave me a fright! Do you always creep up on people like that?'

He enjoyed her confusion. 'I didn't creep, and the door wasn't locked; it's wide open as you can see.' He appraised her carefully, in shapeless overalls and with a red and white cotton scarf tied round her head. Strands of hair were escaping from their imprisonment.

As their eyes met, she felt shock run through her and didn't understand why. She turned away and hid her bewilderment. 'You could have coughed or whistled or drawn attention to yourself in some other way!'

His tone was smooth and mechanical but there was amusement in his eyes. 'I'll remember that, next time!'

She fought for self-control and normality. 'I'm almost finished; this is the last room. Is there a special reason for your visit?' She thought about asking him if he'd come to do a valuation, but stopped herself in time. Gillian repaired invisible faults with some extra strokes of paintwork and avoided looking at him directly.

'No, I was just passing; Elizabeth told me the cottage was almost finished. I wanted to take a look; I thought she'd still be here.'

She waved the paintbrush around. 'Well, help yourself!' Gillian tried not to sound unwelcoming. He'd been generous and provided Elizabeth with the security she needed to buy the cottage. Gillian curved her body closer to the wall so that he could pass easily. As he went towards the narrow stairway, her eyes followed his powerful presence. He stood tall and straight, his broad shoulders filling the width of the staircase as he went round the bend and disappeared from sight. She heard his heavy treads on the wooden floors upstairs, the sound of water running in the bathroom, and then he came down the narrow set of steps again. He took a quick peep at the new kitchen, and the other rooms, and came back to the hall.

Stroking his chin, he stopped and regarded her thoughtfully. His pointed attention forced Gillian to show interest. 'Your father did all the work here, didn't he? He's a local builder?'

Puzzled because she didn't know why he was interested, she replied, 'Yes. Dad has a small building firm, and he prides himself in his work.'

He nodded. 'They've done a good job.' He looked at her enigmatically. 'We'll need someone local to handle any urgent repairs up at Towhay, once the conversion is finished. He might even be interested in doing some work for me now. Do you think he would? The specialist jobs have to be done by experts because of conservation standards, but there will be other work, if he would be interested.'

Gillian wondered if he was just trying to pour oil on troubled waters. He probably wanted to get the whole village on his side; that would make his life easier in the long run. Guests might visit the village and he wanted them to hear positive comments, not negative ones. Gillian coloured slightly. 'I don't know; you'll have to ask him.'

He noticed that her eyes reflected some of the bluish paintwork, a mini-ponytail was trying to escape from the scarf, and her slim figure was rattling around in the baggy dungarees. Ross studied her and nodded. 'I will.' He looked around. 'This colour looks good on the walls — and on you.' Unexpectedly, he reached forward and touched the tip of her nose with his finger; it came away covered in blue paint. A smile lit up his face.

The harder she tried to ignore him, the more she wanted to know about him. She was annoyed and embarrassed about her feelings and her brain froze for a moment. She tried to rub off the offending paint but she only succeeded in smearing it even more.

From his expression she guessed that she now looked like an alien.

Without another word, he turned and went out. Strolling down the flagged pathway, she heard him singing *Funny Face* off-key. The sound drifted back to her, where she stood feeling more mixed up than ever before. Really. She didn't even like the man!

★　★　★

Caroline was munching her way through a plate of scones. The two girls had gone to school together, and were still firm friends. Gillian had never understood Caroline's passion for horses and riding, and Caroline didn't understand why Gillian enjoyed making scones every day. Apart from that, they were very alike in their likes and dislikes.

'It's an absolute godsend! I've been looking around for new premises for months. Harris hasn't spent a penny on the buildings since I moved in four years ago. I'm sure the appearance of the place puts customers off.'

'I agree! It just needed repairs and a

lick of paint now and then. I wonder why he's neglected it.'

Caroline tossed her blonde head heatedly. 'He wants to pull it down — it's in the middle of some fields that he wants to use to cultivate crops. The offer from your friend Ross is an amazing stroke of luck. The stables at Towhay are a dream, and in good condition. The boxes need a bit of attention, but there's an old tack room, and bags of space to put in some more boxes if I need them. The horses will think they've trotted straight into heaven!'

Gillian wondered who'd brought Ross Harley and Caroline together. She didn't ask. She drew imaginary patterns on the check tablecloth and looked out of the window. 'Ross Harley is not a friend of mine. Everyone seems to be welcoming him with open arms, but they shouldn't forget that he's a tough businessman who's here to make money.'

Licking strawberry jam and thick

cream from the tips of her finger, Caroline retorted, 'He's not your friend? Your name cropped up pretty often in the conversation!'

'Did it? Just dropping names, to improve his chances with everyone in the community I expect.'

'He's a dishy man, and rich, isn't he? I'm considering dumping David and running after him!' She giggled.

Gillian smiled. 'Oh, get on! David is worth ten times a Ross Harley, and you know it.'

'Not money-wise, he isn't! But you're right of course — my David is a dream; what other architect would put up with my all-consuming passion for everything equestrian?'

Gillian said casually, 'So, you've agreed a deal with Ross Harley?'

She nodded. 'It's one I can handle. I get the stables for a reasonable rent and he expects me to provide a guest with a horse, on request. Ross said he had no objection if the reception finds out if guests might want to ride during their stay, as long as it's done discreetly. If I do get a double booking, I'll use my own horses, or even borrow some.'

'And it'll work money-wise?'

Caroline nodded. 'Apart from the occasional hotel guest, I think the number of regular customers will increase when they see what super stabling facilities I have. Ross is still figuring out where to put parking facilities; people will have to come and go as discreetly as possible.' She checked her watch. 'Someone is due in half an hour; I'd better go. Coming out on Saturday?'

Gillian nodded.

'Good! See you then!'

Caroline hurried out of the tearoom leaving Gillian meditating and wondering how much more Ross Harley was going to directly, or indirectly, change in their village.

3

Elizabeth called at the tearoom. Her eyes were bright, and twinkled as she spoke. 'Isn't it a kind idea?'

Doodling on her pad, Gillian was reluctantly forced to agree. 'Yes, I suppose it is!'

'If we give Ross your sketches of where I want the furniture to go, and we number the furniture to correspond with the sketches, he promises to get a firm he knows to do the removal. I must admit I was nervous about the actual day when I have to leave Towhay, it would be full of regrets and emotion. Ross' offer means I can go on holiday and then move straight into the cottage afterwards; not quite as radical for me!'

Gillian saw the inherent sense of it, and knew it would lessen the wrench Elizabeth would feel if she had to leave the house and move into the cottage a few minutes later. She put down the pen and began to unload the dishwasher. 'It sounds like a very sensible idea. The new curtains are up in the cottage, have you seen them? That firm did a good job.' Rattling the cups, she stacked them in tidy heaps, and looked at Elizabeth. She seemed very perky. Gillian smiled. 'So, you're going on holiday? Where and when?'

Looking a little smug, Elizabeth answered. 'It depends — whenever you have time and wherever we decide to go!'

Gillian stopped sorting. 'Pardon? What has it got to do with me?'

'When I said I didn't fancy going on holiday alone, Ross said why didn't I take someone with me, and I immediately thought of you.'

With her mouth half-open, Gillian looked as surprised as she felt. 'It's kind of you Elizabeth, but what about Something's Brewing? To be honest, I can't afford a holiday at the moment. I had to buy a new cooker a couple of weeks ago and my savings have dwindled!'

Like a child with a surprise, Elizabeth beamed. 'It won't cost you a thing! I want to treat you to a holiday — I can afford it now, and you've helped me so much in the last weeks. Ross has also offered me special rates; we can choose any one of his hotels for ten days.'

She couldn't suffocate an emerging excitement. 'You don't have to indulge me; you know I was glad to help. I can't leave the tearooms at the drop of a hat.'

Satisfaction appeared on the wrinkled features. 'I've already organised that. Your mum agreed to help straight away; you can also count on Jean — she said so, and Margaret Walters said she'd be glad to help too. Between them, they'll keep things running. You deserve a break. What do you say?'

The wind had been taken out of her sails; what could she say? A smile blossomed. 'What a fantastic surprise! It sounds wonderful, but are you sure you want me to come?'

She laughed softly. 'Who else? I could take one of my part-time gardeners, but that would set the village on its ears, wouldn't it! I'd love to have you with me. You won't be tied to me, you'll be free to go off and explore on your own — you know that!'

'Where would you like to go?'

'Well, I'd love to see the castello in Tuscany! What do you think?'

Gillian ignored the idea that she was consorting with the enemy. She decided she wanted to see his castello as much as Elizabeth did, and she'd love a holiday. Ross would be busy with rebuilding tasks at Towhay, so their paths weren't likely to cross in Italy. Wrapping her arms round Elizabeth, she gave her a fierce hug of agreement.

* * *

According to an outdoor indicator, it was 14°C. There was even some sunshine — not bad for November! Gillian relaxed, her enjoyment growing with every passing second. Elizabeth was a very sprightly lady, who competently took charge of her own suitcase, so Gillian was free to concentrate on looking for a placard bearing their names, or the name Castello di Lorenzo. They were soon following a smartly uniformed chauffeur, who'd been sent to pick them up. It was fifty kilometres from the airport to the Castello near Siena. They leaned back, watched the rolling Tuscan countryside pass by, and looked at each other, smiling.

The hotel was a splendid ancient palace. Careful renovation had kept the original external architectural features, and also the interior terracotta floors, ancient furniture, frescoes and old adornments. Their bedrooms were adjoining; beautifully decorated and with awe-inspiring views of the Tuscan landscape from the windows. It was a place to enjoy life to the full.

Their first evening meal in the small, exclusive restaurant was absolutely wonderful — local dishes and local wine. There were only a couple of other guests — perhaps that was because of the time of year, or just because of the price. The staff moved around with silent competence, and the proprietor Daniela, who'd greeted them on arrival, was very efficient, friendly and helpful.

Next morning, when Gillian woke, she hurried to the window to watch the daylight spreading across the fields and hills. She sat in the comfortable cushioned window-seat with her arms wrapped round her knees, and gazed across the countryside. It looked like something out of a painting and Gillian could understand why people fell in love with Tuscany. In the summertime ochre, red and gold would dominate the scene, and the cypress trees lining the roads would stand contentedly in much warmer temperatures.

Next morning they agreed to go to Siena after breakfast: it was only fourteen miles away. When they made enquiries, the manageress immediately took the arrangements out of their hands. The hotel taxi dropped them off near the centre; it would come to fetch them again later. When they'd walked around the centre for a while, they both agreed that Siena was a beautiful medieval town. They wandered leisurely, guidebook in hand and anxious to see as much as they could of attractions. They enjoyed a light lunch in a small restaurant down a side street where language was no problem — everyone seemed to understand a smattering of English wherever they went. The taxi picked them up punctually at the dropping-off point. That evening they were both full of delight of what they'd seen. After another delicious meal and a nightcap at the bar, they parted in high spirits.

On the way to their rooms, Elizabeth patted Gillian's arm and said, 'I hope you're not bored with my company?'

'What a daft idea! You know I enjoy being with you! I'm glad we're planning a quiet day tomorrow. I can have a swim in the hotel's pool, walk down to the village for a look around, and enjoy a paperback in between times. If you feel like joining me, come; if not just relax all day in the hotel! We can go somewhere on Tuesday.'

Elizabeth nodded. 'I'll see you at breakfast! Don't wait for me though — I like to take my time and you're used to an early start. Sleep well!'

'That's not difficult in such luxurious surroundings!'

She was alone in the pool after breakfast. Floor to ceiling windows had replaced one of the walls in what had been the cellar. From window level, the ground sloped gradually up to the flagged terrace running the length of the castello and to the well-kept gardens beyond. Even though the temperatures outside were cool, it was warm inside and the pool tempted Gillian to dawdle longer than she intended. She sat for a while, enjoying a cup of coffee at a small table on the edge of the pool and taking pleasure in the rays of weak sunshine fighting their way through the windows.

She walked down to the village with Elizabeth in the afternoon, and they spent an enjoyable time looking round the small but neat village. The one store was a veritable treasure chest of ordinary groceries and every imaginable unnecessary extravagance. The owner guided them down to the cellar, where they were confronted by shelves filled with all kinds of special wares. Just the smell of it all made Gillian's mouth water. She bought some delicious-looking hand-made chocolates for her mother and the others who were helping out, back at home.

They were less tired after the meal, so they stayed in the hotel's small bar. Others nodded to them politely but Gillian felt that the exclusive atmosphere meant that people wanted privacy, and that was what they got.

Next day they visited Florence. They soon found it to be much busier than

Siena. There was a massive amount of history, art and architecture to see in such a short visit, so they concentrated on some of the best-known attractions. By the time they retraced their steps over the historic bridge with its old shops, spanning the Arno River, they were both tired.

When Gillian told the manageress, that they were intending to go to Florence by train that morning, she'd insisted they use the hotel taxi instead. 'Mr Harley told me to give you all possible help to make your stay a memorable one.'

The hotel taxi picked them up again and they were happy to rest their feet and let the chauffeur do the work. Gillian felt pretty tired, so Elizabeth — three times her age — must be exhausted.

They opted for another quiet day after that, and enjoyed the luxury of the hotel and its facilities. While they were sitting in a small conservatory drinking coffee that afternoon, Gillian suggested,

'We can go on a trip to San Gimignano, or Pisa, tomorrow if you like. Or stay here, or even go back to Siena again?'

Elizabeth waved her hand. 'Do something without me, Gillian. My feet are killing me! It's more sensible for me to laze around here and recover.'

'I'll go back to Siena, then; I loved it there. If you like, we'll go to one of the other places before our time is up. You don't mind me going off on my own, do you?'

She smiled. 'Heavens, no! I'm glad that I'm not holding you back.'

Gillian smiled. 'I'll go by local bus. I don't intend to tell Daniela where I'm going; otherwise, she'll want to supply the hotel taxi again. It'll be a bit of an adventure to find my way there and back on my own.'

'Take your phone, just in case!'

Gillian got up. 'I'm going down the village now, to find out what time the bus leaves. If I can't figure it out, I'll ask someone in the shop, I'm sure they'll help.'

When she got back, Elizabeth had gone to her room, so she decided not to disturb her. She collected her book, went to the visitors' lounge and made herself comfortable.

'Hello, Gillian.'

His voice sent shock waves through her. He'd appeared out of nowhere. Colour flooded her cheeks as she looked up. 'Ross — what are you doing here?' She dragged her attention from his face and noticed an attractive, cool blonde standing patiently at his side.

'We ordered some new furnishings a couple of weeks ago, and I've come to inspect and see if they're up to scratch.'

Gillian nodded and waited for the introduction; it came. 'This is Fiona — Fiona Burroughs. She's my assistant, a director in the company, and a dear friend too!' He threw an arm round the woman's shoulders.

Fiona looked up into his face and smiled back at him, then she held out her hand to Gillian.

Gillian took it politely and said,

'We've already spoken on the phone.'

Fiona nodded. 'I remember. You wanted to speak to Ross, didn't you?'

She was an elegant, slim woman in her early thirties. Her hair was drawn back into a smart chignon; her make-up was flattering, discreet and perfect. She was almost as tall as Ross was, and her fashion sense left nothing to be desired. She fitted perfectly into the background of the exclusive hotels and his lifestyle; they harmonized so well, Gillian decided they must be more than colleagues, or boss and employee. Seeing them together Gillian was even more aware of how well-groomed, and what a good-looking man he was. He was not handsome in the classic sense of the word, perhaps, but there was inherent strength in his face, and something special about his eyes. There was definitely something intrinsically alluring about Ross Harley.

'Where's Elizabeth?' he asked now.

'Resting, I think. We went to Florence yesterday, and it tired her out — I forget how old she is sometimes. We confined it to the most famous attractions in the centre but perhaps it was still too much.'

'And so you're resting too?' He was smiling as he spoke.

Gillian shrugged. 'Everyone needs time out now and then.' She added, a little defiantly, 'And I haven't been lazing around all day; I've been swimming, and walked to the village and back.' As casually as she could manage, she said. 'Your hotel is great, and all the staff are very friendly and helpful. I've never had so much attention in my life before!'

'Glad to hear they're doing their job properly.' He turned to Fiona. 'We'd better find Daniela, and could you sort out the appointment with Carlo? Oh, get her to confirm the appointment with Enzo for me; tomorrow at 1pm.'

His companion nodded and was already turning away. 'I'll fix it now.' With a smile in Gillian's direction, she sauntered off towards the reception area. Ross was still standing. He viewed her thoughtfully.

'I'll book for a table for all of us; this evening, seven-thirty?' Lifting his hand and not waiting for a reaction, he looked briefly and then turned away.

Gillian had been too startled by the sudden suggestion to utter an objection. She thought about his introduction; Fiona was a 'dear friend' and the two of them were obviously close. If his girlfriend was with him, Gillian didn't mind sharing a meal. She paused and wondered why she agonised over the knowledge that he belonged to someone else. She didn't particularly like him. The only problem was that there was something about Ross Harley that heightened her senses, and it had been like that ever since the day she'd set eyes on him. Some instinct told her to avoid him because he upset her equilibrium, and the feeling remained — Fiona or no Fiona.

★　★　★

She needed to boost her confidence. Until now, she'd worn either a floral dress or a smart trouser suit. This evening Gillian decided to wear the only really evening-type dress she had with her. It was of chiffon lace in shades of sea-green. The colour enhanced her eyes, underlined the ivory tone of her skin and skimmed her slim figure. It always made her feel good. She took special care with her make-up and completed the outfit with high strappy sandals.

She knocked at Elizabeth's door.

'Come in!'

Gillian did, and found Elizabeth was putting on some pearl earrings and adjusting a pearl necklace on her champagne-coloured silk blouse. She looked at Gillian. 'Well, we both look pretty good this evening, don't we?'

'I hope our host appreciates our efforts.'

Elizabeth laughed. 'I'm sure he will. You look lovely; that dress really suits you.'

Gillian gently stroked the soft material. 'Unfortunately I don't get much of a chance to wear it.'

'You don't go out enough. Ever since Ken!'

'I was blind, and caught up in the excitement of having a boyfriend who was the local heart-throb. I should have realised he wasn't to be trusted. Serve me right. But I haven't retreated into a shell! I go out often.'

'But only with the old crowd — you don't meet any new faces.'

Gillian smiled at her. 'Don't worry about me Elizabeth. If I never meet Mr Right, I'll still manage to be happy. You are.'

'But I did meet Mr Right — fate decided, not me. Luckily, I had Towhay to fill my life. I want you to have all the things I didn't, like love and a family!'

Gillian caught her shoulders. 'I love you; I'm your family. We're here on holiday in a wonderful hotel and about to have an evening meal with its owner. Let's just enjoy ourselves, and let the future take care of itself.'

4

Ross and Fiona were already waiting. Ross was wearing a midnight blue suit and Fiona was dressed in a fitted emerald suit in a heavy silk material. She wore her hair up to show long earrings that caught the light.

Ross seemed genuinely pleased to see Elizabeth. The warmth of his smile was mirrored in his voice. He smiled at Gillian briefly, when a waiter pulled out her chair for her, and her pulses began to race. Elizabeth and Fiona were already exchanging small talk; Elizabeth knew her well because of the sales negotiations, so the two of them felt quite comfortable with each other.

Gillian buried her head in the waiting menu, although she didn't really care what they ate. His voice cut in on her diversionary manoeuvre. 'Will you all trust me to order?'

They all nodded. With a hint of humour, he added, 'Good! I must say this is a red-letter day — three females and all of them agreeing to leave it up to me.' He beckoned the waiter, and referring to the menu, he gave their order.

Was it just her imagination, or were the staff more attentive than usual? At any rate, the meal was delicious. Eventually they finished with coffee.

Gillian was light-headed enough to be glad to balance out the alcohol with some caffeine. The conversation drifted to encompass all kinds of things, including Towhay, and Gillian found there was nothing she could really dislike about Fiona. She wasn't snobbish, she was intelligent and she tried to include Elizabeth and Gillian in the conversation whenever she could. She didn't monopolize Ross' attention either.

Gillian tried not to look in Ross' direction, and she tried not to pay special attention to the way Ross and Fiona harmonized. She sat back, joined in when appropriate, and swum through a haze of questions about how she felt about Ross Harley. She was almost glad when Elizabeth folded her serviette and got up. Gillian could join her and thank Ross politely.

His dark eyes were expressionless when he said. 'Are you sure? I thought perhaps we could share a nightcap in the bar.'

She managed to meet his eyes and smiled weakly. 'Speaking for myself, any more alcohol and I'll fall over in a heap. Thanks; another time, perhaps?'

She needed to get used to the idea of Ross Harley and Fiona Burroughs as a pair, even though she shouldn't care, one way or the other. The idea niggled in her head and in her heart.

★   ★   ★

Next morning after breakfast, she set out for Siena by jumping on the local bus. Elizabeth was determined to have a quiet day, so it was a perfect chance for

Gillian to explore the town in more detail again. If she was away from the hotel, she also wouldn't need to see Ross and Fiona.

In Siena, the black and white marble cathedral was her first target. She'd seen the exterior with Elizabeth, now she explored the inside. The Ospedale Santa Maria della Scala was almost opposite the cathedral and she spent time there looking at the frescoes and the works of art in the basement. Back out in the weak November sunshine again, she wandered around the Piazza del Campo with its fishbone-patterned red brick surface. She was fascinated by all she saw. Gillian decided to walk down a side street from the Piazza, intending eventually to have a cup of coffee away from the main tourist haunts. There were small exclusive shops bordering the road, with lots of beautiful wares on offer. She fell under the spell of a shoulder bag with a shiny chestnut surface and a twist-catch, and treated herself.

With her new purchase carefully stored inside a cloth bag, and in a carrier bag, she wandered on and stopped in front of a window displaying local landscapes. There were some beautiful pictures; one in particular caught her eye, a small one that mirrored the colours of Tuscany as it probably looked in summer. A medieval town was on a gentle hill in the background, olive or wine terraces dominated the foreground, and a winding road lined with cypress trees led past them up to the town. Gillian looked at the price tag and calculated quickly. She sighed; it was beautiful, but very expensive.

'Anything in particular you like?' The voice made her body stiffen.

Gillian looked sideways to find Ross studying the pictures in the window too. Startled, she wasn't very welcoming. 'What — what on earth are you doing here in Siena?'

'I had an appointment; someone is covering some chairs for us. He has his workshop at the end of this street. I came out, and saw you standing here looking spellbound!'

She recovered her composure. She should be getting used to him popping up out of nowhere — he seemed to do so continually. Her glance returned to the paintings. 'They're lovely.'

'Which one in particular?'

She nodded in the direction of the small canvas. 'I really like that one. I like it very much!'

He followed her eyes. 'I agree; that's what Tuscany looks like on a hot summer day. Why don't you buy it, if you like it?'

She tossed her head. 'Because I can't afford it!'

He shrugged indicating her carrier bag. 'But you've been shopping!'

'A shoulder bag; it was too much of a temptation. I purchased that without any pangs of conscience.'

He looked at his watch. 'I was on my way to a small café not far from here. I'm due at the bank in an hour. Would you like to join me perhaps?'

Gillian reasoned that if he only had time for a quick coffee, there was nothing wrong with them sharing. She nodded. 'I was about to have some coffee too. Thank you.'

'Good!' Tucking his hand under her elbow, they continued on down the narrow road; it was little more than a wide alleyway. He let his hand fall when they faced oncoming pedestrians and were forced to walk single file; Gillian was glad. She noticed he was wearing casual clothes; beige slacks, soft shoes and a light jacket. They were clearly expensive; but today he looked more like a tourist and less of a shrewd businessman.

'Do you like Siena?'

They'd reached a small café with two small tables on the pavement. He gestured her inside, and after greeting the owner behind the counter and ordering two coffees, he led the way to a corner table.

Gillian answered him as they went. 'I

love it! This is my second visit so far. I think I like it more than Florence. Florence is absolutely beautiful, but it's so bombastic. I'm sure that it's as wonderful and inspiring as everyone says it is, but the atmosphere here in Siena is more my sort of thing.'

The smiling proprietor placed some cups of hot, steaming coffee in front of them and then quickly departed.

Ross drew his cup towards him and stirred the contents restlessly with a small silver spoon. The fragrant aroma encircled them. He nodded. 'I know what you mean. Florence is unbelievable, there's so much art and history. You need lots of time to see it all. There's plenty of art and culture in Siena too, but it feels more informal, intimate and familiar. It's my favourite city in Italy, that's why I looked for a hotel near here.'

She looked up and experienced perplexing emotions as she met his eyes. 'Your hotel is really lovely; well run with a cosy atmosphere.' Gillian reasoned there was nothing wrong with telling him that — it was the truth. 'If you do half as good a job on Towhay, I'm sure Elizabeth will be pleased.'

His mouth curved into an unconscious smile. 'It was never my intention to spoil Towhay — it won't be a family home any more, but we'll be keeping it alive. It was in danger of neglect — and when that goes on for too long, the work involved to bring it up to standard again would be too expensive and too intensive. It almost never pays to convert a building if the substance has drifted too far downhill. Towhay is still in pretty good shape.'

Remembering all Elizabeth's efforts through the years, Gillian kept her cool and took a sip of her coffee before she said, 'Elizabeth has worked very hard all her life to keep it going. She had limited finances.'

He played with the bowl of his cup, and Gillian's eyes were drawn to his long fingers. She looked up and met his eyes as he replied, 'I'm sure, but investment is always essential, as well as necessary care — if not, problems just build up, and too much money is needed to bring things up to scratch.'

She gave him a hostile glare. 'She did what she could, because she loves the house. I'm sure she's the first person to admit she wishes she'd had more money. If she had, you wouldn't be the owner of Towhay today.'

Feeling slightly better, she remarked, 'It must be very demoralising for you to always be making decisions based on money and success.'

He shrugged; a hard edge crept into his voice. 'Success doesn't come easy, and money doesn't either.'

Gillian shook her head. The sunlight had already added faint highlights to her hair. 'I want my teashop to be successful too, but my family and friends are more important to me than my business. I could do without my teashop, but not without my friends and family. I don't think you think like that, do you? Money and profit seem more important to you than anything else. Money rules your life!'

His curt voice lashed out and his eyes flickered dangerously. 'For a very good reason! My father has a small farm in north Wales. Because of various things that all happened at exactly the same time, he nearly lost it. My mother, my sister and I had to go without lots of things for years, things that other people took for granted. Dad managed to pay back the bank loan, but eventually his health suffered and he had a heart attack. After that, I vowed I would never be without money!'

Her lips thinned with anger. 'It's understandable for anyone to want security, but not if it robs you of your sense of objectivity. How much money does one person need?' She wondered why they were suddenly in the middle of an argument.

His features hardened. He leaned back and the chair creaked slightly under his weight. The dark chocolate eyes still viewed her angrily. 'However much it takes; and I haven't lost my sense of objectivity.'

'And what about your girlfriend, the one who married someone else, because you were too busy — was that objective behaviour?' As soon as it was out Gillian realised she'd gone too far. She looked as dismayed as she felt. 'I'm sorry! I shouldn't have said that, it was unkind of me. I don't know why I said it; I'm not usually so rude.' The colour left her face.

Cold eyes sniped at her, and his expression was thunderous. 'I don't know where you got that information, but it doesn't really matter. If we are playing at psychoanalysts, I'll remind you, you're someone who was recently dumped by her boyfriend and I presume your verbal attacks are your way of taking revenge on the world in general, and for some reason I'm also in your line of fire. I'm not responsible if you're frustrated!'

How did he know about Ken? Gillian spluttered. 'I'm not frustrated and he didn't dump me; *I* dumped *him*!' Her breath burned in her throat and her face grew hot with humiliation. She got up. 'There's no point in wrangling with each other, is there? We clearly see life from different perspectives. Thanks for the coffee! Forgive me for getting too personal just now. It wasn't my intention — I got carried away.' As a parting thought, she added, 'But I still don't understand why anyone finds that chasing money is the most important thing in their life.'

'That's because you've been spoiled, and led a sheltered, happy, untroubled childhood. You just can't imagine what it's like not to have money, and how that changes your whole attitude.'

Getting more furious by the minute, she uttered, 'I am not spoiled!'

He merely answered with a knowing smile. Gillian turned and left.

Ross ran his hand through his hair, lifted his hand in protest, feeling suddenly deflated. He got up and reached into his pocket for some Euros.

It was too late to go after her; by the time he had paid, she'd already be down one of the side-streets and lost to his sight.

★ ★ ★

Gillian stopped for a while in a doorway, feeling as if the breath had been squeezed out of her. Why had she attacked him like that? It was none of her business what he thought, or how much money he made. Her cheeks burned at the memory but she had only told him what she honestly thought. It wasn't wrong to be honest, was it?

After making several wrong attempts, she eventually found her way back to the Piazza del Campo, and strolled around for a while just taking in the atmosphere. The pleasure had gone out of her visit, but she bought some postcards at a small kiosk, which also supplied her with stamps. She brooded on whether the heated exchange with Ross had been necessary. Finally, she shook off the thoughts and tried to appreciate the liveliness of the town and its inhabitants. They gestured generously and their voices rang out with a vivacity that was missing in colder climes. She looked at her watch; she had time to catch the next bus if she hurried.

Sitting in a half-empty bus, the route seemed almost familiar because she was already able to pick out some places along the way. On the outskirts of Siena, the bus stopped at some traffic lights and a four-wheel drive with the hotel's logo drew up alongside. She looked down and met Ross' glance as he casually looked up at the bus.

Even if she'd wanted to duck out of sight, she didn't have time to do so. She gripped her plastic bag tightly. His eyes were hidden behind sunglasses, and he gave no sign that he'd seen her, although he must have. Her own forced smile died on her face when the traffic lights changed colour and he accelerated away behind the car in front of him. Although she strained her neck to trace his progress, he was soon just a spot on the horizon. She wondered what he was thinking.

Gillian stared out at the passing scenery and straightened her shoulders. What did it matter what he thought! She didn't need him. He was paired up with Fiona, and he was someone who measured his priorities by the size of his bank balance.

Back in the hotel, she didn't find Elizabeth immediately, so she went to her room. She knocked on Elizabeth's door when she was ready to go down for the evening meal. Elizabeth was ready and waiting and she joined Gillian in the thick-carpeted corridor. In the lift, Gillian said casually. 'I met Ross in Siena; we had coffee together.'

'Did you? Did you enjoy exploring the town again?'

'Yes, I hadn't realised just how much I'd missed when we were on our first visit.'

Elizabeth nodded. 'Good! Ross told me he'd seen you. I met him, when he and Fiona were on their way out.'

'Out?' Gillian queried.

'Yes, they were just leaving. They're catching the late flight back home this evening.'

'Oh!' Gillian didn't know whether to be glad that she wouldn't have to face him, or to be sorry that she couldn't restore their normal relationship. In the end, she decided she was probably glad he'd left, and taken his girlfriend with him.

In the restaurant, Gillian asked her companion, 'What about going somewhere tomorrow?'

Elizabeth shook out the pristine white serviette and laid it across her lap. 'Yes, I think I'd like that. I feel quite my normal self again. Where would you like to go?'

'We could go to San Gimignano, it's famous for its medieval towers, or we could go to Pisa. You choose!'

Elizabeth viewed her and her eyes

sparkled. 'Let's go to Pisa — they've all heard of the leaning tower in the Women's Institute. I'll be able to impress them with that.'

Gillian laughed. 'Right! Pisa it is!'

5

Gillian looked out of the bay window across the village green. Apart from the lush dark green evergreens, most other trees were almost skeletons — and the wind was tugging away determinedly at any remaining leaves. She looked up, and saw that the sky was full of dark angry clouds. A stout man, with his head down, and groping vainly at his flying scarf, came round the angle of one of the buildings. Gillian adjusted one of the curtains, and turned back to the cosy atmosphere of her tearoom. The weather might not be good, but it was good for business. Most of the tables were occupied and a comforting smell of coffee and fresh baking wafted around. She'd recently introduced toasted sandwiches and soup into the menu, and they were popular additions. Her mother was great at making soups, and she filled big saucepans with various kinds that usually lasted Gillian a couple of days. The toasted sandwiches were relatively simple to produce; she just had to be sure there was always enough tomatoes and lettuce available, the other contents could be bulk-bought in advance. In this kind of weather, the added extras were going well.

She cleared empty tables, cleaned surfaces and thought how Tuscany seemed very remote once more, even though it was only days since they'd returned. Elizabeth had moved straight into her cottage when they got back, and seemed to be doing well — in fact, Gillian thought she was glad she had so little to care for, in comparison to her sprawling former family home. She could lean back and relax, join in with village happenings, and not have a bad conscience if she slept late.

Ross had called to see Elizabeth a couple of times — Elizabeth had told her so — but Gillian hadn't seen him, and she wished she didn't feel somehow disheartened by the fact. Why should he call on her? Their last meeting had been far from affable.

The bell tinkled and her dad strode in. 'How's my best girl?'

Gillian grinned. 'As you only have one daughter, I will take that with a pinch of salt.'

He smiled back and kissed her forehead. 'Cross my heart, and hope to die! I need a cup of tea and, as your mother is out buying new clothes, I thought I'd sweet-talk you into providing me with some food and drink.' He looked around. 'Things okay?'

'Umm! Plenty of customers, thank goodness!' She busied herself with filling a teapot and arranging some cake on a plate. She looked around. 'The rush is over for now. I'll join you for a bit.'

Roger Churchill sat down at one of the tables and waited. He was tall, angular, beardless, and with friendly eyes and a kind face. Gillian joined him with a loaded tray, and watched as he speedily devoured her cake. 'How are things with you?'

'Couldn't be better. We've plenty to do, thanks to Ross Harlcy, and some other jobs from our usual customers waiting too.'

Gillian's interest increased. 'What exactly are you doing for him — Ross?'

He took a sip of tea. 'There are specialist firms up at the house, handling the kind of work where they have to be careful because of protection laws — and quite honestly, we'd be out of our depth there. We're renovating a couple of the outhouses — turning them into a flat for him.'

Surprise heightened her voice. 'A flat? You're making him a private flat?'

He nodded. 'Apparently he has a flat, or a couple of rooms, in each place he's bought. He visits all the hotels continually and he wants privacy, away from the bustle of the hotel. In the case of Towhay, the old outhouses provide a perfect starting point to make him a flat. Some posh architect drew up the plans and I'm doing the work. They've come up with some classy ideas! It'll be real stylish when it's finished; two bedrooms, open living room/dining room, study, utility room and a big kitchen.'

'If it's providing you with work,' Gillian said, 'all the better!'

He took a gulp from his cup, and held it in his roughened hands. 'It's not just that — he's offered me a service contract. That will give me some more stability in the years ahead. You know how it is; I'm either chock-a-block with work, or clutching at straws to keep things going. A service contract will help fill the gap sometimes.'

Her father leaned back into the farmhouse chair and it creaked under his weight. 'Know something? At first, I thought he was just a hard-headed entrepreneur — and he is, of course — but I've grown to like him because he's honest and you know where you stand. If he doesn't like something, he says so. He's also able to make spot decisions about things, which makes my life a lot easier in the long run. I don't know what's been happening in the house, but I do know that he follows the work in the outhouse carefully, and there's no pussy-footing around.'

Gillian nodded. She couldn't help prying. 'How is progress, inside and outside of Towhay?'

'From what I see and hear, everything is going well. This isn't the first time Ross has used these firms, and they want to keep him as a customer. They tell me the hotel will be up and running before Christmas. Apparently, they don't intend to open it officially to visitors until the New Year, but there will be a kind of opening celebration before then. Ross's flat will be finished by Christmas, too.'

Hesitating, Gillian asked. 'Dad, was I a spoiled child?'

He looked at her in surprise and shrugged. 'Hard to say! I don't think so, but we always tried to give you what was within our means. We only had you and Brian so you two were probably better off than some of the other kids in the village were. A lot of families round about had more kids and much less income. Why do you ask?'

She looked out the window and recalled Ross's remarks. 'Oh, I was talking to someone recently and they said they thought I'd been pampered.'

He reached forward and ruffled her hair. 'You didn't turn out too bad, whether you were spoiled or not. You care about other people and you work hard; that's what matters!'

★ ★ ★

A week later, Gillian looked down at the ornate invitation to the unofficial opening. Did she have grounds to refuse? Did she have a reason not to go? No, she didn't, and she would go, even if it was only to support Elizabeth.

Other people from the village had received invitations — the vicar, her parents, the local doctor and several others. Since her father had told her about Ross's private flat on the premises, Gillian had grappled with the idea of Ross and Fiona living just a short distance away, and decided she could accept it — not that she had any other choice. They probably wouldn't join in with village life anyway.

Ross had passed her in his BMW on his way through the village a few days ago; he'd beeped the horn, and waved. Gillian had responded and felt relieved. Even if he wouldn't forget her outburst in Siena, he was clearly prepared to disregard it. Like her, he'd probably decided it might be awkward if they avoided each other all the time.

He was an attention-grabbing man and she admitted that, if circumstances had allowed it, she would have been interested enough to want to know him better. One thing stood in her way — she was not going to try to steal a man who belonged to someone else.

Ken had hoodwinked her and led a

double existence with other girls, until Caroline had been caring enough to tell her what was going on. She'd been blinded by Ken's popularity and charm, but when she ended their relationship she was surprised to find how little she really cared. She didn't feel heartbroken, and she realised she'd been in love with love, and not with Ken. It changed her whole attitude. She was more sceptical now — less carefree, and more careful about relationships. She also doubted if she'd ever find real love.

Over the next couple of weekends, Gillian redecorated the kitchen after the teashop closed on Saturdays, doing a little at a time. There was a lot to move around, and little space to deposit things elsewhere — other than in the actual tearoom. She did a wall at a time, so that everything was back in place by Monday afternoon. She didn't want to close the teashop and lose money just to paint. When it was finished, she liked the cheerful yellow tones, the stacked array of china, gleaming cooking utensils, and her green plants on the windowsill. Everything had been thoroughly cleaned in the process and all looked spick and span. Deep down, Gillian knew that decorating was merely a pretext to stay at home; she was turning into a bit of a recluse. At the moment, it was a problem for her to be part of a happy crowd, and she had never enjoyed the forced jollity that was rooted in too much alcohol. She felt uncertain and unsettled; but she was sure she'd find her way out of her apathy eventually.

★ ★ ★

Gillian had taken care with her appearance; a smart dark green tunic dress with three-quarter length sleeves skimmed her figure and brought out the colour of her hair and the bluish-green in her eyes. Daylight was fading when she called to collect Elizabeth at her cottage. They walked companionably to the edge of the village and up the narrow, well-trodden pathway meandering along the edge of the field up to the crest. They paused and looked down on Towhay; it was silent and peaceful. The house was fully illuminated and although Gillian had seen it hundreds and hundreds of times through the years, it had never seemed quite so beautiful. It was like something out of a picture book. It had withstood the passing of centuries, and survived where other houses had been razed to the ground. They stood side by side, staring wordlessly for a moment.

'Do you mind very much?' Gillian didn't have to explain what she meant.

Her hands thrust deep in her pockets and her scarf snugly around her neck, Elizabeth shook her head. 'I've got used to the idea. It will always be mine in my heart, even though I don't own it any more. I had to do what was best for Towhay while I could. Randall never cared or developed an attachment, so there was no point in leaving it to him.

He would have just let it run to ruin. I kept inviting him here when he was young, in the hope that it would ignite a spark of affection for the place, but it didn't work. The only appeal it has for him is its value. He didn't rebuff the idea for a moment when I told him I was going to sell it; he was only interested in how much I'd get. I promised him a third of the selling price now, and he'll get what's left of the rest when I die!'

Gillian looked downwards. The stubble had now been ploughed under, but there was a firm strip of earth along one side — a pathway that went towards Towhay, or beyond to the next village. Local people used the route regularly, just as they had for centuries. The hedges were bare, the birds were silent and the surroundings were soundless.

'Let's get it over with! If it gets too much for you, or if you feel upset, just say, and we'll leave.'

'Oh, it won't be a shock. I've seen most of what they've done already. I'm curious now to see it with all the furnishing and fittings in their place.'

Gillian was more than a little surprised. 'You've been there already?'

The slender silhouette next to her in the semi-darkness nodded. 'Ross took me there occasionally, to show me what was going on, and to ask my advice. At first, I wanted to resist, but then I realised he was doing me a favour. It was a bit of a shock to see the rooms being pulled about, but every time I went, things improved and I could tell they were trying to preserve what they could without losing sight of their own aim — of turning it into a first-class hotel. Of course I wish Towhay could have stayed in the family, but fate has decided otherwise, and at the moment I don't think it is in bad hands.' She moved off ahead of Gillian, along the path winding downward into the darkness. When they reached the bottom, they walked around the building and went in by the brightly-lit main entrance.

There was a lot of activity and a hum of voices everywhere. Gillian looked around and was pleasantly surprised. The entrance hall had been left intact; there was no 'hotel feeling', it still felt like a private home. Gillian saw through a half-open door that the office and reception facilities were in an adjoining room that had formerly been a small pantry. There was a lot of Elizabeth's familiar furniture still in place everywhere. They had been augmented when necessary by carefully chosen pieces that fitted their surroundings perfectly. The old, threadbare curtains everywhere had disappeared and been replaced by heavy rich brocades in shades of green and red. The original dining room was still a dining room, but the long refectory table had disappeared, and a couple of skilfully decorated small tables stood waiting for the first guests to arrive.

As soon as he spotted them, Randall came to tuck his arm through Elizabeth's; she was the guest of honour, and

Randall always enjoyed being in the limelight. Elizabeth gave Gillian a reassuring nod, and Gillian was free to leave her and wander off to examine everything at will.

There was a plentiful supply of food and drink, and smartly dressed waiters offered the contents of their silver trays to the visitors. Gillian knew her way around the house better than most people, and she was curious to see what had been done, if the old house's charm had been lost in the renovation process. Towhay had always been a fairly dismal place when daylight faded, but now discreet lighting everywhere brought out the richness of the wood, the splendour of the proportions and the wealth of craftsmanship of bygone centuries.

Gillian had to admit that Ross and Fiona had done a splendid job. She knew that Fiona was mainly responsible for the interior fittings and decorations, and she'd achieved a clever combination of comfort, beauty and authenticity.

A peep into the busy modern kitchen with its steel surfaces convinced her that it was somewhere the chef would be able to produce meals par excellence. Even now, there was a crowd of people busily replenishing the trays of appetisers and opening bottles of champagne.

She mounted the fine staircase, with its heavy handrail topped with carving. Looking downward, she studied the crowded room for a moment, and saw Ross near the open fireplace with logs burning brightly. His arm was draped casually around Fiona's shoulders. It wasn't hard to pick him out, even in a large crowd like this; he was one of the tallest men present. He laughed at something and his white teeth sparkled briefly. The sound caught her attention and it pleased Gillian. He looked up, caught her eye briefly, and gave her an almost imperceptible nod. She gave him a hesitant smile and turned away.

When she reached the upper floor, she walked down a long corridor embellished with panelling. A Persian carpet, in brilliant shades of reds and blues, ran its length. Small side tables with decorative flower arrangements brightened the way. She opened the door to one of the bedrooms — it looked out over the back of the house. She approved of the luxurious and classy decoration. Anyone would feel happy and contented in luxurious surroundings like these. The bed-linen, the pale carpeting on the ancient planking, the antique furniture and the tasteful arrangement of it all — it was perfect. She crossed to the door that led to the former dressing room, and was now the adjoining bathroom. It was a dream in gold and white, with fluffy white towels and every possible extravagance.

'And? Do I get your approval?'

She looked back across the room. Ross was leaning nonchalantly against the doorframe, his arms crossed on his chest.

'You've done it again — I didn't hear you coming!' Gillian gave him a hesitant smile. 'Yes, I approve whole-heartedly. I haven't seen anything to disapprove so far. I'm glad you've managed to keep Towhay's atmosphere intact. I congratulate you — and Fiona. You've done a good job.'

He smiled at her words of praise, and something tingled in her stomach. It didn't take much for this man to upset her balance. She closed the bathroom door and faced him again.

He tilted his head. 'I saw you coming up here. Your parents arrived a while ago, and your father asked me where you were, so I came to fetch you. I guessed you might be more interested in the changes than most of the people who are down there, but you are welcome to come and do a full tour any time you like. Most people are usually more interested in the champagne and the tit-bits than in the transformation.'

Her colour heightened. 'Well — most of them aren't attached to the place like I am.' She paused. 'Thanks for easing Elizabeth into this new situation, Ross.

She told me you'd shown her what was going on from the very start. That was a good idea. I think that it has helped a lot.'

He brushed her words aside with a slight gesture. 'I like Elizabeth and I wanted her to be able to let go of the place as easily as possible. She must feel a pull, but she even helped Fiona settle some dilemmas sometimes. No one has as much knowledge about the history and furniture of this place as she has. It helped Fiona to have her around.' He gave her a lopsided grin. 'If she was fifty years younger, I'd snap her up as our expert on Elizabethan and Jacobean embellishments.'

Gillian approached him slowly. She hadn't yet worked out how to pass him politely and get back out into the corridor; his sizeable width and stature filled the doorway. She hoped he'd automatically make room when he noticed her approach, but he didn't and she came to a sudden halt in front of him. Her heart thudded as she looked up at his face and she made an effort to settle it back to its natural rhythm. She didn't succeed.

'I'm glad to have the chance to say I hope I didn't offend you too much during our last conversation. Sometimes I'm too honest and I don't stop to think that I may be stepping on someone else's toes. I think I may have jumped on yours!'

He shrugged. 'We were both too heated, and we're both independent characters. Even though we may not always agree on everything, perhaps we ought to just agree to differ sometimes? I wasn't exactly civil to you either, was I?' An easy smile played at the corner of his mouth. 'I was only worried in case we'd end up looking for battleaxes!'

Their closeness was like a kind of drug and her heart took a perilous leap. His gaze travelled over her face and then moved over her body slowly. The smouldering flame she saw in his eyes startled her and she couldn't help wondering what it would be like to be crushed within his embrace and to feel his lips on hers. Gillian wished for it, but when he suddenly gathered her into his arms and held her there snugly, she heard the warning bells in her head.

She ignored them. She ought to wrench herself away from him and this situation. There was no time. Her thoughts were shattered by the hunger of his kiss. It sent the pit of her stomach into a wild swirl. Her lips were still warm and moist from his kiss when she managed to meet his eyes; she could only feel how the touch of his lips on hers had sent a shock wave through her entire body. He held her from him for a fraction of a second before he kissed the tip of her nose, then her eyes, and finally her soft mouth again. Her mind told her to resist, but her body was fighting that advice with every fibre of her body. She caught sight of one of Fiona's beautiful flower arrangements in the corridor and it brought her back to earth with a thud. She managed to push at his chest slightly and get past him without further explanations. She hurried down the corridor, not looking back and resisting the need to touch the lips where his kiss was still burning.

She rushed down the stairs, her colour heightened, and with a feeling of guilt. Should she have protested? Was she to blame for what happened? She smoothed her hair and tried to get some logical thoughts into her brain. She had to find her parents first, act as if nothing world-shattering had happened, then find Elizabeth and persuade Randall to make sure he would deliver Elizabeth to her door at the end of the celebrations. Only then would she be free to leave. She searched the room and found her mother talking to one of the other women on the sidelines of the crowd.

Susan Churchill smiled at her daughter. 'There you are. Dad and I were wondering where you'd got to.' Her mother was evidently enjoying the evening. She had a chance to wear one of her recent purchases, and the dress showed off her good figure and the blue of her eyes.

Gillian seized a glass of champagne from a passing waiter and gulped down the contents in one mouthful. Her mother looked at her in surprise but decided to say nothing.

Gillian steadied her thoughts and answered. 'Oh, I was just taking a look at the bedrooms and the new bathrooms upstairs.'

Her mother nodded. She was looking over Gillian's shoulder and waved. Gillian turned, and found that Fiona was nearby, cuddling a toddler in her arms. Fiona looked happy and contented. The toddler was making an attempt of a return wave with its chubby little hand, and Gillian's mother responded again. Gillian knew how fond her mother was of all children, so that didn't surprise her. But the sight of Fiona with a toddler did. 'Whose little boy is that?'

'Fiona's, of course. He's a lovely little chap. I've been playing Lego with him in the corner while Fiona did the rounds. He's no trouble; he's very adaptable and he played happily with me for ages, even though I'm a complete stranger and the surroundings are strange.'

'Fiona? Fiona has a baby?'

'Um! I think she said he's two and a half. She clearly adores him. He has wonderful dark eyes. He's already a charmer and I won't be surprised if he turns out to be a lady's man when he grows up.'

Fiona gave Gillian a smile as she caught her eye. Gillian managed somehow to smile back, and looked at the happy little boy in Fiona's arms. She felt that someone had just hit her in the solar plexus with a sledge hammer. It wasn't just because Fiona and Ross had a son, although that was bad enough, it was because Ross had come upstairs a few minutes ago, to find her and to kiss her — and these two were waiting for him down here! Her feelings were already confused, and now she also felt thoroughly angry about how he'd used her.

How dare he! How could he cheat on Fiona like that? He must think she had absolutely no moral principles to give in so easily. She needed to get away; from him, from Towhay, from this evening, and from the other people here, as fast as she could.

She looked around until she spotted Elizabeth and Randall and edged her way through the crowd to them. Gillian was aware that Randall had always admired her, and she'd always discouraged him. He wasn't someone she liked much; he was too self-confident and vain. He wanted to stay in her good books, so it wasn't difficult for her to persuade him to make sure Elizabeth got home safely.

Suddenly Gillian spotted Ross coming down the stairs, and his eyes were raking the crowd. Their eyes met for a moment; his were dark and unfathomable, hers were hard and stony with anger. He started to make his way towards her, but she turned determinedly away. She was grateful when she realised that people were hampering his progress with various questions and words of congratulations. It gave Gillian the time she needed to make a dignified exit.

She told her parents that she had a headache, and said goodbye. She hurried down one of the corridors, grabbed her coat, and then left by the back entrance. One part of her never, ever wanted to see him ever again, but another part longed for him. She knew it was illogical, and wrong because he was an adventurer. His kiss was still burned in her memory and that memory was too sweet to simply sweep under the carpet.

She hurried up the path, through the field blanketed in darkness, without taking much heed of her surroundings. It was bitter cold, and the air was sharp and clear. Normally she would have chosen the longer way home, via the road — but she was too mixed-up to think about meeting a shady character on the way. Her breath was ragged. The moon was full and looked like a frozen ball. She increased her pace, wanting to get back to her little flat as soon as possible.

Ross was cheating on Fiona! Gillian hadn't lost anything — he'd never belonged to her — but she felt that she'd now lost everything she'd always wanted. She now knew she loved Ross Harley, even though he was clearly a cheat and a womaniser.

6

Next day she stood rigidly, gripping the telephone and listening to his voice. 'Where did you disappear to, last night? I was hoping we'd share a glass of champagne — if you could manage to forget your reservations about whooping it up in such decadent luxury, of course.' He chuckled and sounded almost exuberant.

She stood there tongue-tied for a second, unable to respond.

'Gillian? Are you still there?'

She pulled herself together, and felt slightly better when she answered. 'Yes, I'm here — I didn't disappear, I chatted a bit and then I went home. I had a bit of a headache.' Unknown to him, the colour deepened in her face and her heart raced. Just hearing his voice just made her feel all mixed up and confused again.

'Fiona told me she'd seen you briefly, but she didn't speak to you, and she didn't know where you'd gone.'

Gillian snapped her mouth shut and took a sharp breath. 'Yes, I saw her too.' Gillian looked for a way to end the brief conversation. 'I have to go, Ross; the tearoom is very busy.' She eyed the half-empty tables. 'I'm glad that the opening went well for you and Fiona.'

'Umm! Don't work too hard! I'll see you after Christmas?'

'After Christmas?'

'Elizabeth has invited me to dinner; she said you and your parents would be there too. She suggested we should all give each other a small gift — to prolong the festive celebrations. I'll have to ask her about exactly who will be there — so that I have the right number of presents.'

'Oh, yes! The Saturday after. I'd almost forgotten. She's only inviting a couple of people. The cottage is too small to seat a lot of guests.' She was uncertain if she really wanted to know, but she asked anyway. 'Will Fiona be coming?'

'I don't think so, although Elizabeth did invite her. Timmy makes things more complicated to for her to accept spontaneous invitations. She's a very organised person, and she also revels in her mother role, so she tries to balance between her working and private life. Timmy's a good kid, and she gives him extra time whenever it's possible.'

Her body stiffened. The bland way he talked about Fiona and Timmy left a sour taste in her mouth — how insensible could one get? 'Sorry! I have to go; we're very busy and some customers are getting very impatient!'

'Have a happy Christmas!'

'You too — and naturally Fiona as well, of course.' She put down the receiver and leaned against a nearby wall to try to recover. Neither of them had referred to their kiss, and she still couldn't get over how blatantly unconcerned he was. She couldn't comprehend how easily he was chatting to her, talking about Fiona and his son, having no pangs of conscience while doing so.

★ ★ ★

By the time Christmas came, Gillian was pretty tired. They'd been busier than usual in Something's Brewing because so many people came to the village, or were in transit to the nearby town, to do their Christmas shopping. She loved the bustle, the Christmas decorations and the Dickensian atmosphere. The weather was not wintry — it rained too often — but a downward trend in the temperatures was forecast for the actual Christmas week, so everyone hoped that meant snow.

Gillian organised a mince pie and sherry party for her friends a couple of days before Christmas. She felt she'd been making mince pies forever, but managed to win great praise when she arranged plates of them and other titbits all around the room. All and sundry were anticipating the special joy of Christmas and family festivities, so it wasn't hard to make the evening a success, and send all her guests home full of the spirit of the season.

Christmas was wonderfully relaxing. Gillian went to her parents early on Christmas morning and helped her mother prepare the meal. Her brother arrived in plenty of time with his wife and two children, and with the turkey already in the oven, and all the vegetables ready and waiting to be cooked, they all traipsed through the cold air to squash themselves into the benches of the church and join the other village inhabitants to sing carols and listen again to the wonderful message of Christmas.

Having two small children in the house when the presents were opened was magical, and brought back memories of Gillian's own childhood. She wondered what Elizabeth was doing at that moment. To her surprise, Randall had picked Elizabeth up to be with him at his home for the day. Gillian hoped Elizabeth wouldn't spend all of her time cooking in the kitchen. She didn't want to think about where Ross was, or what he might be doing.

The days following Christmas Day were filled with the feeling of having eaten too much, and done too little. Her brother and his family stayed for a couple of days, and her mother was practically in heaven, having her two grandchildren at hand to spoil and indulge.

Gillian visited Elizabeth a day or two later, to help her with the shopping for her coming dinner party. Gillian's small car was bulging at the seams when they returned. Gillian insisted she'd make the dessert, Gillian's mother promised to bring the appetizers, and Elizabeth was free to concentrate on the main course.

On Saturday, Gillian left her flat early, to lend Elizabeth a hand with the preparations. There had been a soft sprinkling of snow overnight; just enough to turn the world white. Gillian thoroughly enjoyed the walk to Elizabeth's cottage through the glittering frostiness beneath a sky that was cloudless and dark blue. She carried a tray of tiny individual desserts in small glasses. Each one was different and had small amounts of various fruits, sponges, blancmange, rich cream, mousse, jelly, chocolate, and creamy yoghurt. She'd spent lots of time decorating them, and if they tasted as good as they looked, everyone would be satisfied.

Elizabeth had told them all to bring small presents to exchange with one another, so Gillian had a rucksack full of small packages on her back. She pretended she hadn't taken special care to pick out something for Ross. In the end, she'd chosen a beautifully illustrated history of the Medici family.

Elizabeth could seat eight people round her dining table, so she'd invited Gillian, Gillian's parents, Ross, Randall, and the vicar and his wife. Gillian tried not to think about Ross, and was determined to keep her distance. There wouldn't be much room for anybody to move around once they were all seated. Gillian positioned herself near the kitchen door, to help with the serving and clearing. She also placed Randall at her side.

It was almost dark when the others began to arrive. After the initial greetings and a glass of sherry, they all moved into the small dining room area. During the initial conversation and gossiping, Gillian had to stop herself giving Ross any kind of special attention. Instead, she concentrated on Randall, who was clearly flattered. He was delighted to be seated next to Gillian. Ross retained his affability, and she almost felt jealous when she noticed how the vicar's wife was giving him her whole attention, but there was a distinct hardening of his expression as the evening progressed and he watched Gillian and Randall.

Elizabeth viewed the young people

with surprise. She loved Gillian dearly and thought she knew her well, but today Gillian's behaviour puzzled her. Eyeing Gillian and Randall chatting like closer-than-close friends, Elizabeth guessed that it had something to do with Ross, as Gillian had been unnecessarily reserved with him all evening.

Elizabeth's first dinner party in her new home was a success. That fact should have made Gillian happy, but she was suffering under the strain of being in the same room as Ross. She needed to demonstrate that she didn't need him, and that she didn't want him.

There was much laughter when the presents were exchanged. The men ended up with socks, handkerchiefs, aftershave and the women unwrapped scarves, books, and bath-salts. There were a few curious glances when Ross handed Gillian a beautifully wrapped package. Gillian opened it to find the small oil painting she'd seen in the shop window in Sienna.

She stared at it, speechless. The other

guests did not realise how costly it was, of course, but she did. 'I — I can't accept this, Ross!' she stammered.

'What? You don't like it any more?' he drawled with more than a touch of mockery in his voice.

'Of course I do, but this is not what I call a 'small' gift!' She found herself starting to colour as a hush descended around the table briefly.

He shrugged. 'I saw it was still in the window a couple of weeks ago, and rcmembered that you'd liked it. Would you have preferred to receive lavender bath-salts?'

Gillian gave in. 'I love it, of course.'

Almost as if he was relishing her discomfort, he said, 'Then enjoy it — a souvenir of Tuscany, from me!'

She was reluctant to protest further with the others half-listening. Perhaps she'd get a chance to return it discreetly at some time in the future. She did love it; the colours brought back the magic of Tuscany to a frozen English country- side. Ross had already turned away to chat to the vicar's wife.

After the meal, they all re-assembled in the small sitting room and the conversation ran in all directions. No one noticed that Gillian was unusually quiet. Randall sat on the arm of her chair and was pleasantly surprised to find Gillian didn't throw off his arm as he draped it casually round her shoulders. Gillian tried to avoid any eye contact with Ross. As time went on, the stiff expression on his face grew stronger and Randall's proprietary behaviour increased.

Gillian tried hard not to think about Ross; he had no right to judge her. He had Fiona and a son, he was cheating — she was single and unattached. She was free to choose who she wanted as a boyfriend. Randall had never been an aspirant, but today he filled the gap and unknowingly helped her get through the evening.

Gillian barely noticed the discussion about recent political happenings. She was glad when the vicar and his wife stood up and initiated the process of leave-taking. Gradually all the others stood up too and began to gather their belongings, prior to departure. Before he left, Randall kissed her on her cheek. Gillian had always tried to block similar moves in the past — but Ross was still around and watching, so she tried to look pleased.

Randall raised his hand. 'I'll be in touch, Gillian.'

Gillian didn't reply, but Randall was still feeling so smug that he didn't notice. He sauntered off down the hallway and to his car, parked in the lane.

Gillian had listened to him brag about his new Mercedes sports car all through the evening — he was obviously already making inroads into the money he'd got from Elizabeth. Gillian wasn't sorry to see him go.

Ross was the last in line to leave. Thanking Elizabeth politely for an enjoyable evening, he said, 'I'll keep in touch.' He turned to Gillian and hesitated for a moment. 'Would you like me to see you home?'

Flustered and torn by conflicting emotions, she replied. 'No thanks! I'm going to help Elizabeth clear things before I go — but thanks for the offer.' She was mesmerized by his dark eyes and her mind was whirling.

Elizabeth suddenly noticed that the vicar's umbrella was in the hallstand. She left Ross and Gillian and hurried down the pathway, waving the umbrella energetically above her head.

Ross studied her face for a moment and Gillian was immediately unnerved. Her stomach knotted, and then he surprised her by saying softly. 'Don't worry! I get the message!' He turned on his heel swiftly and hastened down the bricked pathway to his BMW.

Gillian's parents and the vicar were still standing and outside the cottage gate saying goodbye as he murmured goodnight to them again. The wheels of Ross' car spun loudly on the tarmac as he drove off into the night.

When she came back indoors, Elizabeth was clearly pleased with how the evening had gone. Gillian listened with one ear and nodded as they cleared the table. She was glad to be occupied. If she'd gone straight home, she would have moped and dwelt on things.

Helping Elizabeth to wash the dishes might distract her; things might return to their proper perspective. Half-heartedly, Elizabeth suggested leaving everything till next morning, but Gillian sensed she was glad when Gillian suggested doing the washing up straight away. Elizabeth could take her time to put her beautiful crockery and cutlery away tomorrow. Gillian soon had her forearms in the soapy suds.

Brandishing a tea towel, Elizabeth chatted cheerfully. 'You seemed very friendly with Randall this evening. I thought you didn't like him? Even if he is my great nephew, I didn't think he'd stand a chance in the same room as Ross Harley.' She picked up another one of the dinner plates and began to rub at it vigorously.

Swilling the next plate and standing it on the draining board, Gillian answered. 'I'm not the least interested in Randall. You know that — '

'Then what was wrong between you and Ross tonight?' Elizabeth cut her off in mid-sentence.

Gillian answered curtly. 'There is no 'me and Ross'. Ross Harley is Fiona's partner and they have a son.' She paused. 'I like him, and he senses it. I wanted him to grasp that I'm not up for a cheap affair on the side. Admittedly I wasn't fair to Randall, because he was just a means to an end this evening.'

Elizabeth stopped and stared at her, her eyes wide and taken aback. 'Ross and Fiona? A son? Don't be silly! Where did you get that idea from? Fiona is married to David. He was at the opening — he's a really nice man — tall with blond hair, standing next to Fiona all evening. Tim is *their* son! Ross and Fiona are old friends. Fiona has worked with Ross from day one, and they've worked hand in hand in Dreamhotels ever since, but there's nothing emotional about their friendship in that way, and I'm certain about that.'

Gillian nearly dropped the plate she was holding. She was glad she could put it down unharmed into the dish rack. She stood there, her mind a complete blank for a moment — then surprise and shock took over. The colour faded from her face; she stared into the darkness of the small back garden. She managed to utter some words. 'I — I assumed they were lovers when I saw how well they got on, then I saw Fiona with the little boy. No one ever told me he was Ross's son — I just put two and two together!'

'And made five!' Elizabeth held out her hand for the next plate. 'Why didn't you ask me or someone else before you jumped to the wrong conclusion? Ross owns Dreamhotels, but Fiona has the status of a director and is paid accordingly. David is an accountant, and I think he's in charge of the accounting side of Ross's business, and that isn't an easy job, because of the various international placements. Fiona and David have been married a couple of years and David is able to work from home and keep an eye on Tim if Fiona is away. They have a housekeeper and Fiona's mother lives nearby, so Tim is well cared for.'

Gillian was still in a daze and she stared at Elizabeth wordlessly.

Elizabeth eyed her and gave a soft laugh. 'I wondered why you were acting so strangely. I was surprised that you were clearly avoiding Ross but I couldn't figure out why.'

She took a quick breath and then Gillian nodded. 'I thought he belonged to Fiona and was determined not to let him think I was ready for the taking.'

'Well you can easily put things right. Tell him you got things mixed up.'

Gillian was scarlet. 'And show him what a complete idiot I am? If I explained, it would be paramount to admitting I fancy him!'

Elizabeth gesticulated with the tea-cloth. 'And . . . would that be wrong? Naturally, it's up to you, but if you don't, you'll just remain a casual friend from the village — like all the other people he already knows.'

She felt dumbstruck by her own stupidity and wondered if she'd have the courage to put things right without appearing to be brainless or to be chasing him. Why had she assumed Ross and Fiona were lovers? Looking back, she had to admit there were no signs of loving affection. There was deep friendship, but no romantic passion.

She'd deliberately pushed him aside. How did she explain it was all a big misunderstanding without looking like a predatory female? Perhaps she'd now lost the chance of ever being part of his life. The bitter realisation gave her a sense of loss. She'd looked at the Tuscany painting with pleasure, but it now also made her feel bereft and desolate.

7

When the teashop reopened, business was sluggish. People ordered less cake as they began to think about post-festivity dieting. Gillian juggled with mundane things like how many scones to make each day, what choice of cake to display, or when she should get round to removing all the tinsel and glitter. Monday was her day off.

Caroline and her fiancé, David, had been working hard renovating the stables at Towhay since before Christmas. The stalls had been repaired and repainted, the tack-room had been cleared and cleaned, and everything was looking very neat and orderly. Caroline phoned Gillian to suggest they could go for a ride together as things were slack up at the riding stables and she knew it was Gillian's day off.

Gillian hadn't talked about Ross or

her dilemma to Caroline. For the first time in her life, she was reluctant to talk to her best friend about something so important, but the problem was too special to even share with Caroline.

Gillian wasn't an enthusiastic rider, and Caroline always gave her one of the gentler horses which was accustomed to unpractised riders. Once they were on their way, Gillian was glad she'd come; it was pleasant to be out in the fresh air. Following behind Caroline, the two of them went through the nearby woodland where the leaves on the well-trodden pathway made a dry, brittle sound beneath the hooves of their horses, and where the previous year's bracken blanketed the ground in large patches of brown everywhere. It was very quiet and they were alone with the trees and the cold wind. There was frost on the ground, glittering in places where the morning sunlight hadn't reached. They came out of the shelter of the wood and climbed a gentle hill in a shallow curve, up to the remains of an ancient ruin. It must have been a magnificent place in bygone times. Now it was neglected, and deep shadows between the remaining buttresses gave it a gloomy aura.

Back at the stables, she helped Caroline to groom the horses, and they shared a mug of coffee. Sitting on a bale of hay, mug in her hand, Caroline studied her friend's face. 'Is something wrong? You're very quiet. You didn't seem to enjoy Alan's New Year's party very much either.'

'Oh, but I did!' Gillian gave a weak laugh. 'No, nothing's wrong; just a touch of winter depression like millions of others. Winter is not my favourite time of year! I'm looking forward to everything turning green again.'

Gillian decided it was high time to pull herself together. If Caroline noticed she was down in the dumps, other people would too, and she didn't really have any reason to be miserable — she had a good life with no real problems — apart from wanting Ross Harley. 'I enjoyed our ride together this morning. It was just what I needed — getting out into the fresh air and pumping some extra oxygen into my bloodstream! Jolly is such a gentle horse; he's lovely.'

'Yes, I agree, everyone likes him. He's good for beginners.'

Gillian laughed. 'Like me!'

'Oh, you're not a beginner any more, but I've given up hope that you'll ever turn into an enthusiastic rider.'

Gillian put down her mug and hung up her hat on a convenient peg. 'I'm off! I promised Mum I might go shopping with her later on, and I want to do some washing first. Thanks! Perhaps we can meet up on Saturday evening?'

'Yes, I'll be in touch.' Caroline was glad to find her friend wasn't completely in the doldrums after all. She got up too. 'I'm going to wax the saddles. Once the hotel opens and the weather improves, I might not have much spare time on my hands.'

Gillian nodded and lifted her hand as

she exited. She zipped the neck of her anorak tighter around her neck and thrust her gloved hands deeper into her pockets. In her close-fitting jeans and long boots, she made an attractive picture. Her heels sounded on the cobbled stones as she made her way towards the driveway. She was halted in mid-step when she heard him.

'Gillian!' Gillian turned and colour flooded her cheeks. She managed a polite smile, although her insides were raging at the unexpectedness of seeing of him again.

'Ross! I thought we wouldn't see you very often — now that Towhay is finished. I thought you'd only come if something goes wrong.'

In a few strides, he was at her side. 'And probably you pictured me with a whip in one hand a flail in the other — all kitted out to flog the life out of any insubordinate employees!' He smiled mischievously. His eyes twinkled.

Gillian barely reached his shoulder

and had to look up at him. The wind was messing his thick hair. 'Don't be silly!' she said lightly. 'Although technically you probably are our lord of the manor now — how annoying!'

With tongue in cheek, he replied, 'I promise not to take advantage of my position.' In a more serious tone, he said, 'I do the rounds of all the hotels at regular intervals; Towhay is one of them now. You can talk to managers via the phone, but generally speaking, it's better to check things yourself. Sometimes a chat with a member of the staff or some of the guests can tell you something is going wrong before it gets to be a real problem.'

Gillian nodded and looked up into his dark eyes. His face was already stamped on her memory and he continually inhabited her dreams, but she still studied Ross as if it was the first time she'd ever seen him.

'I'm not here because of the hotel though; I came back to check the progress of my flat. Some new furniture has been delivered this week.' If he was annoyed with her because of the other night, he'd either adjusted, or chosen to ignore it. In any case he gave no outward sign of displeasure.

'My dad told me about it — about the flat, not the furniture!'

'Would you like a guided tour, or have you seen it already?'

'No, I haven't. I may be plain-spoken but I'm not cheeky enough to intrude without permission, even though I admit that I'm interested and curious. My dad keeps telling me how stylish it is. He's finished, isn't he?'

'Yes, a week or so ago, and he and his crew did a terrific job. Once all the workers were out, I ordered the furniture and fittings, and now it's almost reached the final stage. It looks very good, even if I say so myself. Just as I hoped it would be. The kitchen hasn't been installed yet, but most of the other furniture is in place. I'll show you around, if you like.'

They strolled round the angle of one

of the buildings towards a group of former outhouses. As she walked alongside him, Gillian thought she ought to explain why she was here this morning — there was no official reason for her to be wandering the grounds of Towhay any more. 'Today's my day off and I've just been for a ride, with Caroline,' she offered.

With his hands deep in the pocket of his Barbour jacket, he looked across at her with interest. 'Do you like riding? I didn't know that!'

She pushed back a wayward strand of hair and spoke in a casual jesting way. 'I enjoy it now and then, as long as I'm with Caroline! I've never been passionate about it. I usually ride Jolly, he's the horse Caroline normally reserves for children. I can manage him.'

The corner of his mouth lifted and there was teasing laughter in his eyes. 'I think that horses always sense who's in control from the word go, so it's sensible not to overestimate your abilities. Perhaps Jolly is cleverer than anyone imagines. He carries light-weights most of the time, kids who probably adore him, he isn't expected to jump high fences, or wide brooks and the like, and he probably gets more exercise than most of the other horses because he's so uncomplaining and philosophical.'

'Do you ride?'

'Occasionally, but not very often. Growing up on a farm, it was one thing we did have that other kids didn't — ponies. But I don't have a lot of spare time, and until now it was always a bother to find a nearby stable. Perhaps I'll go for a ride more often in the future, now that your friend has her stables here.'

Ross slowed his pace and gestured towards the open door of one of the old outhouses.

Although the outward appearance of the squat buildings had changed very little, once they were inside Gillian didn't recognise the place. The space had been beautifully utilised, and as she looked around, she felt proud that her dad had been involved. After the tour, they ended up in the living room with its soft leather furniture, modern storage units and neutral light colours.

'Wow!' She turned to him. 'It's great. Who would have thought anyone could make so much out of a couple of old storerooms?' She admired a large, modern picture on one of the walls with its vague outline of a group of women in brilliant red, blue and yellow dresses. 'That's a beautiful picture. Just right!'

He looked pleased. 'I think so, too. The rough texture of the wall is a perfect background for the smoothness of the painting.' He gestured vaguely and ran a large hand through his thick hair. 'I wish I could offer you something to drink, but the boxes haven't been unpacked yet. I can't even offer you a coffee until the kitchen is installed.'

Gillian brushed his remark aside, and went on with her assessment. 'The furniture and pictures are all very modern, but it still harmonises really well with the building.' She paused imperceptibly, decided to plough on, but didn't get to finish her question. 'Did Fiona . . . ?'

He smiled and shook his head. 'This is my choice, all of it! I leave the hotels up to Fiona, but I make my own decisions about what goes into my private habitat.'

Gillian looked around. 'Well it's lovely! Why do you want rooms in each hotel? Surely you're never able to live in them for long?'

'No, but I still like to have a feeling I'm coming home, and living my own life when I'm off duty. If I had a house somewhere, it would automatically increase my travelling time, because most of the time it would never be at hand. Rooms or a flat are an ideal solution. It's an added expense, but the flats could be incorporated into the hotel for self-catering, if I didn't need them any more.'

'Lucky you! I have enough trouble

keeping up with the mortgage repayments for Something's Brewing. The prospect of having to keep up with running and also the financial aspect of your hotels is mind-boggling.'

He smiled. A tumble of emotions seized her and she felt hypnotised by his arresting looks.

'That's where Fiona's husband comes into it. He's a bit of a financial genius. I trust him implicitly; he keeps the financial side of things strictly under control, and keeps me constantly informed of where I stand. Naturally, I'd hate to see any of the hotels go down the drain, but if something does goes wrong with any of them, only the weak one would suffer. We've safeguarded each hotel on its own merits so that if one hotel fails, it won't automatically drag the others down with it.'

Gillian nodded. She was glad that he didn't seem to bear any ill will about Elizabeth's festive dinner party. He had the right to be angry and ignore her thereafter. While she looked at him she searched around for a logical, plausible explanation.

She didn't need to rummage around in her brain for long, because he beat her to it and put her in the picture. He spoke with quiet determination. 'Elizabeth told me you thought that Fiona and I were hitched — that you didn't know she was married to David?'

Her breath seemed to have solidified in her throat and she fought to control her swirling emotions. She hoped her smile looked noncommittal, but she knew the colour in her face had heightened and that she was still feeling uneasy. She managed to speak. 'I assumed that, from the day you came to Castello di Lorenzo with her. I don't know why, I never asked; I just presumed so; probably because the two of you seem to get on so well.'

'We do! And that was why you tried to deliberately keep me at arm's length the other evening — just because you thought I was tied to Fiona?'

She swallowed hard and nodded;

what was the point in pretending?

'In the beginning when you came here, I didn't really trust you because of what you represent, but later I thought you and Fiona were a couple privately as well as professionally and I thought you weren't being fair.' Her blood pounded and she turned a vivid scarlet. 'When you kissed me, I thought you were cheating on Fiona.'

He stood looking at her with a quizzical expression for a moment. Ross studied her wide eyes, fine high cheekbones and her mouth with a resolute set to it. He ran his fingers through his hair. 'What a waste of time.'

Knowing what he meant, Gillian nodded again automatically, musing on everything she liked about him. His movements were very economical and indicated that he was a man who had things under control; his face and body were devilishly handsome, and he was a successful businessman with a clear-cut character. She didn't agree completely with his attitude, but wanting to be successful and being ambitious weren't really bad characteristics.

His square jaw tensed visibly and then softened. 'I think it would be an excellent idea if we start from scratch again, don't you?'

Her face mirroring her relief, she rewarded him with a smile. 'What a good idea!' She held out her hand. 'How do you do? My name is Gillian Churchill. I'm very pleased to meet you Mr Harley.'

His hand met hers in a warm clasp and he chuckled. He drew her towards him and his lips brushed hers as he spoke. 'Thank Heaven for Elizabeth! Do you realise we might have gone on avoiding each other for the rest of our lives, if she hadn't put me in the picture?' Then his mouth descended on hers, and it was warm and sweet.

Gillian was shocked by her response; the feeling of his lips on hers was a delicious sensation. His kisses were as rewarding as they were challenging. He held her close, and then taking her shoulders, he declared, a note of delight in his voice, 'Let's meet up away from this place, and get to know one another a bit better! I really hate to say so, but I have to leave for north Wales straight away. I should have been on the road a couple of hours ago, I have an important appointment this afternoon — but this morning, after Elizabeth told me about you mixing things up, the temptation to find you and sort things out was too great. I was just on the way to your teashop when I met you.'

She felt ridiculously elated.

'Do you ever close the teashop?'

'I'm usually closed on Mondays, like today. There's not much going on after the weekend.'

'So you have Sunday and Monday free?'

'Yes.'

'Come up to London on Sunday. I'll get tickets for a show, and we won't have a problem filling in the rest of the time either. If we met here, all eyes would be riveted on us; you're too well-known locally. What do you say?'

He gave her a smile that sent her pulses racing. 'I'd like that.'

He nodded. 'I don't own a hotel in London, but I know several people who do. I'll book us some rooms.' Looking briefly at his watch he said almost apologetically. 'Look, I've never been sorrier, but I have to go. I've an appointment with a council surveyor, and if I get into his bad books, it would be fatal. I wish I could stay for a while longer, but I can't — I'll make up for it next Sunday, all right?'

Gillian felt too happy to say anything other than, 'Yes, of course.'

To her delight he kissed her quickly again. 'I'll phone you tomorrow!'

He let go of her to grab his briefcase and an overnight bag. Gillian walked with him to his car, where he gave her a farewell kiss. Her emotions were out of control when she kissed him back and then stepped back to watch him drive slowly down the driveway. Stopping at the wrought-iron gates, Gillian saw the shadow of him waving his hand before he turned on to the main road, and she heard him roaring off towards the motorway.

8

Travelling on Sunday, it was quiet everywhere. Ross met her at the station. Gillian felt a bubbling excitement when she saw him. His gaze travelled over her face and searched her eyes; he seemed satisfied with what he saw. He reached out to take her overnight bag and kissed her on the cheek.

'We'll just go back to dump your things at the hotel, and then we'll go for lunch. There's a nice little Italian restaurant, just round the corner.'

Gillian smiled and nodded. Feeling buoyant, she tucked her arm through his, and they walked to the taxi rank. Generally, whenever she was in London, Gillian was always interested in the surroundings, but today, the view from the taxi's windows wasn't so fascinating. Her gaze wandered back to his face all the time. They exchanged generalities and seemed to feel comfortable just being with each other.

The hotel was small and very exclusive. At the reception desk, everything had already been sorted out. Soon she had a key in her hand and they were in the lift on the way to the third floor. Her instinctive response to his nearness was a purely sensual experience and kindled feelings of fire. Gillian could see he felt relaxed and carefree. It was wonderful to be alone with him. The doors slid open and he waited for her to exit.

'Down to the right, I think.'

Gillian walked and he followed. The room had an en-suite bathroom and overlooked a small park-like area behind the hotel. It was blissfully quiet. He put her bag down and smiled.

'Do you want to unpack?'

'Only my dress for this evening. It won't take a minute!' She extracted what she needed and he viewed it with interest. With her dress hanging in the wardrobe, she turned to him. 'So! I'm

142

ready if you are!'

Ross had been sitting on the corner of the bed, but stood up and looked pleased. 'Let's go then!' He held out his arm and Gillian took it.

On the way down in the lift again, he pushed tendrils of hair away from her cheek. 'I'm in room 207, in case you have to contact me.' He cupped her chin tenderly in his warm hand and kissed her softly.

The doors glided open in the foyer and with a look that sent her pulse rocketing he reached out and laced his fingers with hers. Gillian didn't resist; she was in seventh heaven.

They left the hotel and had lunch. Time never passed so quickly and although the food was mouth-watering, Gillian couldn't even remember later what they'd eaten. The conversation roamed and wandered and there was no trace of awkwardness. A feeling of fulfilment and pleasure encompassed them. She could tell he felt comfortable with her too.

They went for a walk along the Embankment after lunch. It was cool, so there weren't many people out walking, but the sun was trying to break through and the two of them just took pleasure in the surroundings and each other. There was an undeniable magnetism between them and Gillian relished his closeness as he checked his long stride to match hers.

By the time they got back to the hotel, daylight was slowly fading. They went into the small lounge and shared some coffee — to bring warmth back into their bodies, and also prolong the moment when they'd part to get ready for the evening. Ross had tickets for a musical.

They met in the lobby, and he gave her an admiring glance as she emerged from the lift in a heavy silk dress. It had cost more than she cared to think about, but it emphasised her slim figure, brought out the highlights in her hair and showed her legs off to perfection.

'You look wonderful!' He smiled.

Gillian felt drugged with happiness. She studied her companion and returned his smile. 'You look very good yourself.'

It was true. In his midnight blue dinner suit, there wasn't a man alive who could have looked better. She was delighted to be his partner. They waited for the taxi to arrive, sitting at a small side-table, next to one of the three floor-length windows overlooking the street. The weather was dismal and daunting but apart from that, nothing could possibly spoil the evening.

She continued to feel euphoric and Ross seemed pleased with himself too. Gillian decided she was one side of a coin and he was the other. They were so obviously in step with each other's mood. They sat side by side in the theatre enjoying the musical and eyeing each other now and then. In the pause, he fetched two glasses of champagne, and it wasn't just the pale liquid that was fizzy and sparkling; Gillian's insides were bubbling with excitement too.

Ross lifted his glass and gently

touched the side of his to hers. 'Here's to us. I'm really glad you came!'

Gillian was in a state of high excitement. 'And I'm so glad you asked me. To us!'

On the way back to the hotel, they discussed the musical and talked about what they would do tomorrow.

'How about a trip on the Thames? It's not the best time of year to be wandering around outside all day. If we took a bus or a boat trip to some tourist attraction, we'd be indoors most of the time, see something new, and not have to walk miles and miles to do so. Another alternative would be a visit to a museum or something in that line.' His face was partially hidden in the darkness of the cab. 'What time do you have to leave tomorrow?'

Gillian didn't like to think about leaving him at all. 'Seven in the evening. That'll get me there at a reasonable time. I left my car at the station.'

'Good! Then that gives us most of the day.'

'What about you? Are you off again somewhere?'

'Yep! Paris. First thing on Tuesday.'

'Lucky you! I've never been there!'

'Haven't you? We'll have to correct that.'

Gillian didn't comment; she only hoped he meant it. Still feeling decidedly buoyant, and as if she was walking on air, they talked about possible places of interest to visit, and decided to go to Hampton Court. All too soon, they reached the hotel.

In the lobby, Ross turned to her and asked. 'Hungry? Thirsty?'

Gillian threw back her head and gave a soft laugh. 'I'd really love a cup of coffee.'

He reached out, lacing his fingers with hers. They went to the hotel bar where they sat at the bar. They were the only visitors and soft music played in the background. She had coffee and Ross ordered a lager.

'Tell me more about yourself. Tell me about your family.'

Gillian laughed softly. 'You've met mine — apart from my brother and his family. Tell me about yours!'

'You'll have to meet them. That is a lot easier than me describing them!'

The conversation flowed easily, and Gillian didn't want the day to end, it had been absolutely perfect. After a while, she yawned a couple of times, and tried to hide it with the back of her hand.

Ross laughed softly and said, 'Somehow I think it's time to call it a day. It's easy to tell that you're a country girl! Come on!'

Gillian slid down from the bar stool. 'I have an early start every day, so normally I don't often stay up later than midnight. I'm busy long before opening time.'

Ross turned to face her. 'You like your teashop, don't you?'

Gillian nodded. 'Of course, otherwise I would have given it up long ago. I love being with people and I like to think that Something Brewing is a kind of meeting place for local people. I don't make a huge profit, but I get by and I enjoy myself.'

They walked side-by-side to the lift. Inside, he pressed the button and it whizzed upwards with silent efficiency. They walked along the soft-carpeted, silent corridor, and she searched her bag for her key. When she found it, he took it out of her hand and opened the door. Before she could take the last few steps, he'd captured her in the doorway, his hands resting on the doorframe, each side of her face. Her heart galloped wildly.

His breath was warm on her face and her heart raced as his mouth covered hers hungrily. Gillian felt her knees weaken when his hands began to slip down her arms and begin to explore the soft lines of her back, her waist, and her hips. Crushing her to him, he pressed his mouth to hers again and she kissed him back, lingering and savouring every moment. Gradually he edged her backwards into her room and his hand searched for, the light switch. Light illuminated the room. The door was still open although neither of them was aware of it. Her breath was uneven as he kissed her again. He looked her over seductively and the prolonged anticipation was almost unbearable. Gillian was carried along by the moment but she was also the victim of her own rank uncertainty. Her misgivings increased by the minute. She wanted him, but she was suddenly scared he didn't feel strongly about her. Perhaps he was just using her.

She loved Ross, she was sure of that, but what did he feel? He'd never spoken about how he felt, although she knew he liked being with her. Perhaps that was enough for him, but it wouldn't be enough for her. Just a few words of reassurance would have made all the difference, but they didn't come. They hadn't known each other long. Perhaps he was just the kind of man who was more interested in sex than in commitment.

Today was the first time they'd been together for any length of time, and Gillian wondered if he'd organised the weekend with the aim of spending the night with her. She took a moment to catch her breath and to settle her disturbing thoughts a little. Her nerves tensed and a cold knot formed in her stomach. Ross looked puzzled at what he saw in her eyes.

Gillian was recalling Ken; how he'd simply taken her love for granted, how he'd expected that she'd be around whenever he had the time. She also remembered how he'd cheated on her completely in the end. She'd found that she didn't love him anyway, so it hadn't hurt — but it had left scars and a fundamental mistrust. She'd known Ken much longer, and much better than Ross. Why should Ross be different to Ken? Was his weekend invitation just a means of getting her in the right mood for a quick liaison?

He met dozens of women in the

course of his travels. He knew lots of attractive, intelligent, willing females. There was nothing special about Gillian Churchill. She needed time to reorient herself; time to think about him, sort out her feelings, and she needed more time just to know him a little better.

Gillian withdrew from his arms, moved back a step and then remained motionless for a moment. He hesitated, blinking with bafflement. She coloured fiercely when she looked at him again and blurted, 'I hope that you aren't expecting too much, Ross.' She found it was hard to remain coherent when she was so close to him.

'Too much? What do you mean, too much?' His eyes were dark and intense. He waited.

Her breath quickened and her cheeks were warm. He stiffened when she said, 'I'm sure that you know exactly what I mean. I don't intend to jump into bed with you, the first time we go out together.'

There was derision and sympathy

mingled in his glance when he replied. 'I had the impression we were both travelling down the same road; but clearly I misunderstand you completely. I had no intention of forcing you to do anything you didn't feel happy about. I wasn't planning to force you into bed with me.' He clenched his mouth tighter and the skin was drawn tight over his cheekbones. His dark eyes glistened. 'I didn't realise that I was making you feel uncomfortable, but we can soon amend that.'

He turned on his heel and paused. Turning back, he continued, 'I sincerely hope that today wasn't just another performance on your part — one to just make me feel rather stupid again!' He continued towards the open door, and his voice was heavy with sarcasm when he looked back with reproachful eyes and said, 'Sleep well.'

Gillian stood frozen to the spot. Something inside her wanted to yell at him to come back; another part was glad he'd left. She knew that he deserved an explanation, but she hadn't sorted out her emotions fast enough to formulate anything. If she said too much and admitted that she loved him, it would pin him down to making a statement. Gillian knew he liked her, that was fairly easy to tell, but she wanted much more than that. She didn't want to force him into admitting something he didn't feel.

She stood watching him as he strode down the corridor into the waiting lift. He didn't turn to face her again as the lift doors closed behind him. Gillian closed the bedroom door and leaned against it. She slid down its surface and sat on the carpet, staring ahead of her. She didn't know whether she'd acted reasonably, or had been plain stupid. All she wanted to do was to sort out her tangled thoughts and be sure of what she wanted. After her experience with Ken, she wondered if she could ever be happy with anyone.

Next morning, after a sleepless night of tossing and turning, Gillian went down to breakfast early. The room was empty. Monday morning was probably always quiet. She was keyed up to face Ross. She knew she needed to explain that her memories of Ken had come between them, and it had nothing to do with him. She poured some cornflakes and drenched them with milk. A waitress appeared.

'Would you like tea or coffee? Your room number?'

'Tea, please! Room three hundred and five.'

She bustled off again and Gillian stared out of the window.

The waitress returned with a pot of tea and a white envelope. 'Mr Harley left this for you Miss Churchill.' She handed it to Gillian.

Taking it, Gillian automatically asked, 'Has Mr Harley had breakfast?'

The woman nodded. 'He was the

first one down. He gave me that with your room number; as far as I know, he's checked out.' She looked at Gillian with sympathetic eyes.

Gillian was pale before she took the envelope; now she was almost the same colour as the paper. Her voice was halting, but she managed a polite 'Thank you!' She waited until the waitress was out of sight again, looked at her name and her room number written on the front for a second, then slit it open with her finger. It was brief and to the point.

★　★　★

Dear Gillian,

I'm puzzled and feel uncomfortable about last night, but perhaps I expected too much? We seem to end up at loggerheads all the time, don't we? I wonder if it is chance or intention that every time we seem to move a step forward, you take two steps back. Perhaps I was under a false impression from the very start? Evidently, we want two different things.

In a way, it's a pity that you did agree to come, as it has now made the situation more difficult for us both than ever before. It would have saved you, and me, embarrassment if you'd thought things through to the end, decided that we just don't suit, and just turned me down when I invited you to join me this weekend.

I'm leaving for Paris today instead of tomorrow.

It was not my intention to offend you in any way, but I'm not solely to blame. I'll try to keep out of your way from now on, and hope that we can at least get along with each other at a normal level if we do happen to meet. That might happen from time to time, because of my visiting Towhay, but I promise not to trouble or pester you any further!

The hotel bill is settled, so you are free to do whatever you like in London until you catch the train home. Enjoy

*the day and give Elizabeth my regards
when you see her.*

Best wishes,
Ross

★ ★ ★

She couldn't enjoy a single minute without him. Upstairs, she re-packed her bag in a matter of minutes, and caught an earlier train home. The feeling of heartache and loss she'd felt as she watched the passing scenery from the train just seemed to increase and get worse. She felt utterly miserable by the time she arrived home, and went straight to her flat.

Her spirit sank as she re-lived the situation. She'd now never have the chance now to explain why she'd been scared last night. He'd avoid her from now on, and she could understand why. She'd humiliated him with her stiff rejection; he wouldn't forgive. Perhaps he thought she'd just been toying around him purely for her own entertainment.

Gillian felt intensely lonely, but she didn't want to talk to anyone. She hadn't told anyone, apart from her mother and Elizabeth, that she was going up to London to meet Ross, so she wouldn't need to answer many questions about how she'd enjoyed herself over the weekend. Elizabeth and her mother were both much too diplomatic to force her to talk about it.

On Monday morning, she opened the teashop and managed to act normally. No one noticed that her world had fallen to pieces. If anyone had looked closer, they would have seen that she was unusually pale and it cost Gillian an effort to greet customers cheerfully all day. Trying to grin and bear it was tiring, and headache-inducing, but she kept going until she could thankfully lock the door at last and flee upstairs.

She swallowed a lump that lingered in her throat whenever her glance skimmed the picture of Tuscany. She recalled sitting opposite him in that small coffee bar. He'd written that they wouldn't need to ignore one another, but there wasn't a single word of encouragement in his letter. Her thoughts circled and circled around Ross. She could recall every detail of his face, and she remembered the invisible web of attraction that was between them. Her lack of courage had ripped that web into a thousand pieces in a couple of seconds.

She carried on as usual, but her heart wasn't in it. Her heart was wherever Ross was. After withdrawing into her shell for a couple of days, Gillian realised it was making things worse. She decided to go round to see Elizabeth. She had to get out of the flat and divert her thoughts.

9

Elizabeth had settled into her picturesque cottage very well; perhaps she felt reassured, now that the future of Towhay had been settled in her lifetime. She was still able to keep an eye on it, and visit it whenever she liked, for as long as she lived.

Elizabeth busied herself in the kitchen and returned to the cosy living room with a tray of crockery and a plate of home-made biscuits.

Absentmindedly Gillian took one. She looked at Elizabeth. 'Um! These taste good.'

'An old recipe of my mother's; I'll copy it out for you.' Elizabeth paused and looked at her young friend. She was unusually pale and there was no sparkle in her eyes. 'Is there something wrong? You're not ill, are you? Where's that optimistic grin of yours?'

Gillian waved her hand vaguely. 'I'm fine. It's nothing.'

'Come on! Something's amiss! I've known you too long. I thought that I'd sorted out the wrinkles between you and Ross. Come on, what on earth has happened now?'

After a second or two of hesitation, and acknowledging there was no one else, apart from her parents, that she trusted more than Elizabeth, Gillian poured out her troubles. It was a relief to voice them. Elizabeth listened, and viewed her silently until she was finished. 'So you pushed him away, without really explaining that you felt frightened?'

Gillian nodded. 'I know it was stupid, but all those negative thoughts about what happened with Ken shot through my mind, and I got scared. I couldn't expect Ross to define what he felt about me, but I think that was what I needed. I had to know I wasn't just a passing affair. When I felt more rational, I think I could have explained, but by then it was too late; he'd left.'

'Ross is a proud man, Gillian. He probably felt a bit foolish; perhaps he even thought you were playing around with him — to see if you had power over him.'

Gillian looked down at her tightly clasped hands in her lap. Her voice was a little stronger. She could trust Elizabeth. 'I just didn't want to get hurt again. I wasn't sure if he just wanted a good time at my expense.'

Elizabeth wrung her age-spotted hands. 'You're not painting a very flattering picture of Ross's character, are you? Oh, I understand why you felt like you did, but how is Ross supposed to know? Even if he's aware you had a boyfriend who let you down, he doesn't know the details and he doesn't know you have scars, or that it has made you much more cautious.'

Gillian tried to meet Elizabeth's eyes and somehow managed it. 'It's too late now. Why should he forgive and forget? I've treated him badly a couple of times; he must think I'm a complete idiot.' She sighed. 'It probably wouldn't have worked anyway. He comes from a completely different kind of world — it's one of sophistication and rich people, and exotic places. I'm a country mouse with my roots buried deep here in this little village.' She got up and walked to the small window to stare out into the darkness.

Elizabeth sighed. 'What has where you come from got to do with it? I like Ross very much. He's successful at his job, and it's made him affluent. He's worked hard to get there, and he has to work just as hard to stay there. His parents run a small farm in north Wales near one of the hotels he owns; did you know that? He has a sister living nearby. He has his feet firmly on the ground; I'm sure he doesn't measure people by where they come from, what they do, or whether they're rich or not.'

Gillian turned and ran her fingers through her hair. 'See — you know more about him than I do!'

'Gillian, if you have to climb a mountain, then you need climbing boots. If you need to sort this misunderstanding out, and give Ross a chance, you'll need skill and determination. From what you told me, I'd agree that he probably won't make the first move. He has tried a couple of times and you've rejected him. It's up to you now.'

Gillian's eyes widened. 'I can't! I can't run after him. I might not be welcome. I don't know if he does more than like me. Perhaps I'm just imagining things.'

'And you'll never find out, if you don't tell him why you dumped him and give him a chance to respond.' Elizabeth took a sip of tea and put the cup down with a clatter. 'It comes down to whether you love him or not; if you do, you have to fight for him. Do you love him?'

Gillian nodded silently.

'Then basically you have to decide whether you want to go on being miserable for the rest of your life, or not. No one else can unravel the knot. What have you got to lose if you just try?'

'My pride?'

'Hmph! Forget that! Think about how you've chipped away at his pride by pushing him away. Even if he gives you the cold shoulder, you won't have to live with the 'what would have happened' syndrome for the rest of your life. Don't throw away the chance of putting things right; it's the only one you'll ever have!'

Gillian wavered, and the uncertainty was still written on her face. Her thoughts began to hurtle forwards and she began to wonder if Elizabeth was right.

Elizabeth smiled softly. 'Think about it and take your time, but don't wait too long. Every day you wait pushes him further and further away, and makes it harder and harder for you.' She leaned forward and took a biscuit. 'I know. Let's have a game of cards! It'll help to take your mind off things for a while. And I think I have rather a good chance of beating you tonight!'

Gillian laughed shakily and went across to an old-fashioned Welsh dresser filled with old willow pattern dishes and plates. She opened a drawer and took out a much-fingered pack of cards. 'We'll see about that!'

Elizabeth had voiced her thoughts, but she now dropped the subject. Elizabeth had always been the same. She always left it up to Gillian to make her own decisions, and never condemned her if Gillian didn't take her advice. Gillian had always been grateful — there was no fuss, no kerfuffle, just Elizabeth with her own belief and words.

★ ★ ★

It took some courage but a day later, she took Ross's business card out of the drawer and phoned his number. Fiona answered.

'Hello Fiona, this is Gillian. I wanted to talk to Ross. Is he there?'

'Hello, Gillian. What a nice surprise to hear from you. Hope that you're well? No, Ross isn't here, I'm sorry. I'm not really sure where he is at the moment. He had an appointment with some people in Paris on Tuesday, and he phoned to say the meeting had gone well. I didn't think to ask him where he was off to next. He usually phones in to let me know his schedule, but he hasn't done so far. He will, though. Would you like me to ask him to phone you when he does?'

'No . . . no, that isn't necessary. It's not important, honestly! I can talk to him the next time I see him.'

'Well . . . if you're sure? Anything I can do to help?'

'No nothing, thanks. How's your son? My mother is still raving about him. She loves children, and she said your son was a dream of a little boy!'

Fiona laughed. 'She hasn't had to fight him tooth and nail to get him into bed on time — but I must admit, when he uses his charm, he's hard to beat.'

'Well — thanks, Fiona.'

'What for? Sorry that I couldn't help. Nice to hear from you. Perhaps I'll see you next time when I have to come down to Towhay?'

'Perhaps! You're welcome to call at the teashop any time.'

'I'll take you up on that; I've always been too busy. Ross has praised it to high heaven. I'll put it on my schedule on my next visit. Bye!'

'Bye.' There was a click and the connection was severed. Gillian leaned back and couldn't make up her mind if she was relieved because she didn't need to talk to him just yet after all, or frustrated because she still had to find out where he was, and still didn't know how she would formulate her explanation when she finally located him.

Tapping his visiting card against her knuckles, she glanced down at it. Elizabeth had given it to Gillian, when she contacted Ross about Elizabeth's loan for the cottage. Gillian had just tried the printed telephone number, but he'd also written his mobile number underneath in ink. Did she have enough courage to try it? Perhaps Fiona never gave his mobile number to anyone without checking first — it would be a sensible move, otherwise he might be inundated with unwanted calls.

She felt nervous at the mere idea of hearing his voice, and knew she would stutter her way through an explanation like an idiot. Perhaps he would cut the connection immediately when he knew who it was, and not give her a chance? She turned the card over and over. An idea developed in the back of her head. What if she just sent him a text? She could ask him for a chance to explain. She wouldn't need to face him, and he'd be free to consider carefully if he wanted to answer, or not — it would be a lot easier than speaking to him personally.

She took her time thinking about

what to say. Keeping it short and to the point, she sent him the message. *I'm sorry about what happened. I'd like to explain if you'll give me a chance. If not, I understand and we'll forget the episode forever more.* When her finger hit the send button, she still wondered if she was doing the right thing, but it was too late now.

She was on edge for hours afterwards but there was no reply. She left her mobile phone on the shop counter and almost hit the ceiling every time it buzzed. It was always someone she knew, but never any message from Ross. Feeling more deflated than ever, she closed the shop for the day and went upstairs. She had a shower and made herself an omelette. She wasn't hungry, but she'd been dodging meals the last couple of days, and she knew that it couldn't go on indefinitely. She'd fall to pieces if she didn't take more care. Wistfully she looked at the Tuscany picture on the wall of her bedroom, and decided she'd go back there next holiday. It didn't need to be an exclusive hotel, there were lots of typical Italian family hotels; they'd be just as enjoyable. Even if Ross didn't want to talk, he'd still given her a taste of Italy, and Tuscany in particular. She wanted to go there again.

She was just getting ready for bed, when she thought she heard her phone. Looking around, she realized she'd left it downstairs. She clattered down the narrow steps and realised it was still ringing. She dashed forward and pressed the right button.

'Gillian?'

Her breath caught in her throat. 'Yes. Hello, Ross!'

'I phoned a couple of times earlier on, but there was no reply.'

'I was upstairs. I just realised my phone was in the tearoom and I didn't hear it.'

'I've arranged for a flight for you for tomorrow.' There was a rustle of paper. 'With British Airways, leaving at 12.55

arriving 15.10, from Terminal 5. Can you make it?'

'A flight? A plane trip?'

'Yes. I can't get away. I have an appointment tomorrow morning, but I thought if you could organise someone to handle the teashop you could come here. Then we could sort things out faster.'

'Where are you?'

'I'm still in Paris. Can you come?'

Gillian's brain whirled, but she didn't need to be asked twice. 'Yes, I'll come. I'm sure that Elizabeth will stand in at the teashop and I'll get Jean or my mother to help.'

'Good. You can pick up your ticket from the British Airways counter. I hope I've given you enough time to make your way to Heathrow and get through the security checks.'

'I'll try to get the earliest train possible from here . . . and I'll pay for my own ticket!'

'Don't start arguing, or we'll be at loggerheads about that as well! I wish I didn't need to drag you all this way, but I'm stuck, and I won't be able to get away until next week. I'd like to settle things before then, if possible.'

She swallowed and paused for a second. 'I'm glad you're giving me a chance to explain.'

'I'll pick you up at Charles de Gaulle, but if I'm not there for any reason, go to the Hotel de Place, rue Tronchet. It's not far from the Madeleine Church. I'll see you tomorrow?'

Gillian grabbed a pen and wrote the name and address of the hotel on one of the menus. 'Yes, till tomorrow!' There was a click and he was gone. Gillian felt elated and wanted to whoop. At least he didn't detest her. Coming back down to earth again, she looked at her watch and punched in Elizabeth's number. Elizabeth never went to bed early, and Gillian had never been more grateful for that fact than at this moment.

Tomorrow was Saturday, and they closed at three, so Elizabeth and Jean

174

should be able to manage as long as things weren't too busy. She'd get up early and make a couple of batches of scones. She was determined to go; nothing would stop her — even if she had to close Something's Brewing for the day!

10

At Heathrow, Gillian's ticket was waiting, as promised. Once the plane landed in Paris, she went through passport control, and towards the exit half in anticipation, and half in dread. She had packed a few things in a small overnight bag — she didn't know how long she'd be staying, but reckoned it would be at least for one night. She hesitated, looking at the throng of people waiting for arrivals. She spotted Ross's tall figure straight away; her breath caught in her throat and her heart pounded like a jungle drum. Misgivings surfaced briefly again; but he wouldn't have wanted to see her unless he was prepared to give her a chance. Gillian looked more relaxed than she felt as he came towards her. When they met, his expression was guarded and her thoughts floundered again.

Awkwardly she cleared her throat.

'Hi! You made it, then?'

He regarded her for a moment and then reached out for her bag. 'Yes, as you see. Let's get out of here.' He waited until she fell in at his side and then led the way. They went back into Paris by train and roughly half an hour later, they exited the Gare du Nord. They didn't have chance to talk on the way, the train was full and Ross and Gillian sat apart. At the Gare du Nord, Ross headed for the taxi stand and gave the driver the hotel address.

Gillian asked. 'Is it far from here?'

'Roughly five kilometres. Too far to walk.'

In the intimacy of the car, she had to try to shut out the awareness of him, but nothing could stop her longing for the haven of his arms. She pretended to be interested in the sights he pointed out, and it wasn't long before they drew up outside the Hotel de Place. Ross offered his hand to help her out, and she took it, feeling like a breathless teenager. She tingled under his fingertips and wondered if he was aware of the effect he had on her. He bent down to give the driver some money and then turned towards the entrance. 'Just follow me!'

The foyer was quiet, although there were staff ready and waiting to efficiently attend to visitors' needs. The furnishings were clearly exclusive and the whole impression was of a classy, luxury hotel. Gillian ignored the curious glances of the receptionist and someone else in the office directly adjoining the desk. Ross just nodded briefly in their direction. Gillian trailed after him into the lift. He inserted a key in the panel, pressing the top button.

He explained, 'My flat is on the top floor; the lift only goes that far if you have a key.' Unobtrusive classical music played softly in the background, and Gillian nodded. His nearness made her senses spin.

When they finally stood in front of his flat door, Gillian was curious. He unlocked the door, and gestured her in.

It was bigger than she expected, with expensive furniture and fittings in neutral shades of cream and black. Bright paintings and decorative items lightened any austerity. It had a lived-in, comfortable feeling. Wall to floor windows looked out on to a small balcony and across the rooftops of Paris. She moved automatically towards it. 'What a wonderful view! Just like the movies!'

He smiled and her heart lurched madly. 'Yes, I often think I've kept the best part of the hotel for myself. Would you like something to drink?'

She shook her head and cleared her throat. 'I'd like to talk about what happened in London. I want to get it out of the way.'

He nodded and gestured towards a leather couch. She sat down gingerly and he dropped down next to her, with one arm lying inches away from her shoulder. Gillian longed to reach out and grab his hand.

She tried to remember exactly what

she'd planned to say. 'Firstly, I'm terribly sorry about what happened. I didn't intend to humiliate you. I'm sure you felt embarrassed and wondered why I was blowing hot and cold.'

He shrugged, his eyes never leaving her face when he said, 'I presumed that I'd misjudged your feelings.'

Their eyes locked and their breathing was in unison. Gillian waited to give her heart time to quieten, but it didn't, so she ploughed on. 'You didn't misjudge anything. I just panicked because the past took over.'

'The past? What do you mean?' He was puzzled.

Gillian told him about Ken and their short relationship. He was silent and didn't comment. She was relieved that she'd manage to explain at last. 'I was suddenly scared that the same thing might happen again. We don't know each other well, and your lifestyle is completely different. Nobody can ever know how much they like someone in the beginning, but ever since Ken tripped me up, I imagine everyone, you included, might only be interested in a fleeting, casual affair. And I'm not that sort of person.'

His compelling brown eyes, the firm features, the confident set of his shoulders made her waver, but somehow she managed to continue. Looking down at her hands, she said, 'I don't want you to admit what you don't feel, Ross, and I don't expect you to lie either. I just want to explain why I acted as I did. If I'd explained on the spot, I'm sure you'd have understood. You deserved an explanation there and then, but I handled the whole thing badly. It was just a kind of automatic mental reaction — pushing you away had nothing to do with you as a person.'

His voice had a new depth when he reached across and drew her across the couch towards him. 'How silly can you get? You surely know I've been in love with you for ages?'

She stared at him in astonishment

and her features relaxed. Pulling her to him, he pressed her lips to his, and it left her mouth burning with fire. The shock of discovery hit her full force as she repeated, 'You love me?'

He laughed softly, caressing the curve of her back. 'Yes, of course I do.'

Feeling euphoric, she stared wordlessly, then gave herself freely to his kiss. She kissed him back with hunger and drank in the sweetness of their longing. She couldn't disguise her feelings any more, even if she'd wanted to. For a moment, with arms intertwined, they were just contented in the knowledge that they'd found each other at last.

Then Ross said, 'And . . . do I have a chance?'

'Need you ask? Yes, I love you — I've never felt like this before.'

He gazed at her in contentment. 'I'd almost given up hope. I've thought about practically nothing else all week. I love you too much not to have tried to put things right again, but I was still plucking up courage.'

'We're both a bit confused, aren't we?' Gillian bit her lip. 'But I don't really belong to your world. That bothers me still. All your hotels, all this money and luxury — I'm just an ordinary girl running a little teashop!'

He threw back his head and laughed. His large hand took her face and held it gently. 'You are not ordinary, and don't worry about the hotels; they're only buildings; my job. Work is work, you are you; and you are all I want.' With tongue in cheek, he went on. 'And if I ever go bust we'll always be able to fall back on your teashop!'

Her eyes sparkled and her senses were reeling. Another kiss sent new spirals of ecstasy through her. She was coming back to life again. She wanted to be part of his life and always safe like this, in his arms. She answered teasingly. 'Oh — so you're only after my money?'

Ross smoothed the hair back off her face, kissed her nose and replied, 'How did you guess?' He hugged her. 'Let's get some other things out of the way now. I had a girlfriend once, who didn't love me enough to wait. You had a boyfriend who wanted other girls. We both found out what love is not — but it also makes it easier to know what real love is!'

Gillian nodded. 'Perhaps.'

Holding her close, he murmured, 'I am what I am — I won't be able to suddenly lose interest in my hotels, and you'll cling to your teashop, I know that too. We have to accept each other as we are. Perhaps my business was a substitute for what was missing in my life — I now realise it was you!'

She nodded again.

'Once you're really sure about me, we'll marry, and we'll make the flat in Towhay our home. We'll take on the rest of our lives from there. I'll still need to travel, but I will try to reduce it, promise — perhaps I'll train someone else to take over some of the more mundane things. If you're waiting for me at Towhay I think it'll get harder and harder to drag me away. Perhaps you can join me on my travels sometimes? I'm looking forward to showing you the hotels and sharing my life with you — more that you can ever imagine.'

She snuggled up to him. 'Umm! I think I'll love that, not because of the glamour and the riches but because they make you proud.'

'Good! If you can appreciate that, it'll be half the battle. You'll undoubtedly try to pin down my ambitions, but I promise that nothing will ever be more important than you are. If you're really against something, I'll try to fall in line. Promise!'

She was stunned at her own eager response to the touch of his lips. Just his nearness made her senses spin. She knew she could trust him, she could give him her love and know that he would never abuse it; he was the kind of man who kept his word, someone she could always rely on.

He gave her an irresistible grin. 'Let's celebrate! I suggest we stroll around Paris — it's the city of lovers, and we're lovers — even if the weather isn't good today. Then we'll go for a meal at my favourite restaurant, on to a nightclub and after that we'll come back and open a bottle of champagne.'

'Sounds perfect.'

'How long can you stay?'

'I can stay till Monday. Elizabeth and Jean are filling the gap today.'

'That gives us two whole days! Wonderful!' He stood up, pulled her into his arms again and swung her gently around. 'You don't know how many times I've wanted you with me during the last couple of weeks. I've been miserable and blamed myself because I decided I'd been expecting too much, too soon. I thought I'd been stupid, and lost you forever.'

'You're not stupid, you're the most wonderful man I've ever met. I've never been so sure about anything in my life before. I love you, Ross. I always will, and I'll always be there for you, and I'll make you happy if I can.'

He kissed her. 'You're already doing that! Somehow I'm sure we can look forward to a great future together.'

She nodded, and lost herself again in the longed-for intimacy of his arms.

THE END

We do hope that you have enjoyed reading this large print book.

Did you know that all of our titles are available for purchase?

We publish a wide range of high quality large print books including:
Romances, Mysteries, Classics
General Fiction
Non Fiction and Westerns

Special interest titles available in large print are:
The Little Oxford Dictionary
Music Book, Song Book
Hymn Book, Service Book

Also available from us courtesy of Oxford University Press:
Young Readers' Dictionary
(large print edition)
Young Readers' Thesaurus
(large print edition)

For further information or a free brochure, please contact us at:
Ulverscroft Large Print Books Ltd.,
The Green, Bradgate Road, Anstey,
Leicester, LE7 7FU, England.
Tel: (00 44) **0116 236 4325**
Fax: (00 44) **0116 234 0205**

Other titles in the
Linford Romance Library:

TOMORROW'S DREAMS

Chrissie Loveday

Nellie is a talented paintress in the pottery industry of the 1920s. Disaster strikes the family, and she becomes the main breadwinner for her parents and three siblings. But the fates conspire against her and she is forced to seek employment where she can find it. She loses her heart to the wrong man and he, recognising her special talents, offers her a future. But how could she ever move into his world?

TO LOVE AGAIN

Fenella Miller

Since she was widowed, it has been difficult for Emma Reed and her young children, Jack and Mary. But then, Rupert Bucknall offers her a job as his housekeeper. However things do not go well. Rupert has a fearsome temper and doesn't want her or the children to remain. Since his accident Rupert has lived as a recluse, believing his scars make him hideous. But Emma, with nowhere to go, must persuade Mr Bucknall that she is indispensable.

HERE COMES THE BRIDE

Kat Parkhurst

Isobel's sister is getting married and wants her to be a bridesmaid. How hard can it be? Very hard, it seems, as bride-to-be, Kelly, lurches from one disaster to the next. Isobel tries to help, but her own relationship is threatened, her beloved granddad ends up in hospital, and then she has a car accident. She begins to wonder if the wedding will ever take place — and if she would be in any condition to be a bridesmaid . . .

A FAMILY AFFAIR

Catriona McCuaig

The Great War brings sadness for Nurse Emma Meadows and her parents: her brother has an accident while learning to fly a biplane, and after a neighbour spurns her, their young sister runs away from home. Emma, herself, loves Dr James Townsend and when he is reported dead on active service in France she goes there to learn the truth of his death — little knowing what she will find when she gets there.

FOOL'S PARADISE

Teresa Ashby

Karen Scott and her twin brother, Travis, travel to the Virgin Islands to study a coral reef and make a documentary film. However, Karen's fiancé, Jeremy, is furious and breaks off their engagement. Meanwhile, Karen falls for another diver, Ross Allen, but when he finds out about her fiancé back home, he suggests that she still has feelings for Jeremy . . . When the filming is over, will Karen return home with her brother, or will she stay with Ross?

THE GOLDEN LURE

Katherine Langton

Working as companion to a crotchety elderly lady, Ella Matthews' existence is brightened by her brother's letters telling her of his adventures on the goldfields of Australia. When he invites her to join him she's thrilled to go and experience some adventures herself. But arriving in Melbourne, she's stranded, alone and fearing for her brother's safety. The only man she can turn to is journalist Nathaniel Lake. Will he agree to let her accompany him to the goldfields?